The
Fugitive

By Linda Ferguson

Preface

This is a book about the possibility of time travel and the friends that bonded in a way no others had ever or could ever have imagined. The perils and adventures they embarked upon were traumatic, heartfelt, and educationally engaging. There were moments of playfulness, moments of sadness and worry. Tragedy and despair and even death. There is an old familiar face that keeps hope on the horizon when all seems lost. The characters are real and familiar as if you were reading about the kids you grew up with.

Table of Contents

Chapter 1

The Time Capsule

Sitting in a damp, abandoned, fetid, hovel in the outskirts of the city was the last place I ever thought I would be spending my 24th birthday. Hiding like a criminal with childhood friends that will be forever bound to me by something we can never take back.

The year was 2014. I was in my third year at Arizona State University, and still kept up with my same friends. How could we have known this would be the outcome to a question we asked so long ago? A question we thought was as innocent as the children that asked it. "Was time travel possible?"

As I watch the flames dance in the fireplace, I kicked back on a noxious loveseat with a sheet draped over it to keep off the dust. The house was full of sheet draped furniture and tattered drapes hung at the broken windows that were too sullied to see out of. The house looked like it was once a pretty sweet farm house that seemed as though the owner was planning on returning to someday. Two story, white with what was left of black shutters on the windows. Must have been at least forty acres of land around it. Thorny overgrown rose bushes on either side of the rickety porch. The roof has caved in a bit from neglect and some of the floorboards were starting to warp, but enough shelter to keep us warm, dry, and hopefully safe.

Funny, a year ago I might have thought the people who owned it must have died and the family kept it for a tax write off. Now nothing seems simple or obvious. Ever since the day my friends and I put that stupid time capsule in the ground.

Let me start from the beginning. The year was 2009; we were just starting our sophomore year in high school. My friends and I had grown up together in a great community in the north side of Phoenix. There was Brett, who was the clown of the group with his long, slender build and sandy blond hair cut high and tight like a marine and a face only a mother could love. He had a smile that filled your heart with laughter before he ever opened his mouth. He was quite the comedian.

His green eyes were shadowed by his reddish blond eyebrows that matched the single strip of beard that lined the middle of his chin.

Then there was Sammy. I never knew why but for some reason, the girls loved him and he them. He was tall, blond, had buck teeth and a foul personality. Don't get me wrong, he was my friend but he had no filtering system. If he thought it, he said it. He looked like one of those wrestlers on the WWF. He was vulgar in his demeanor and not a shy bone in his body. One might call him a borderline sex addict, a real Casanova. He was the type that could charm the panties off a nun and have her coming back for more. His 6' 4" 200lb frame and eyes as blue as the ocean when the morning sun glistens across it that were irresistible to the ladies. I guess he had a way of making them feel at ease. Made them feel beautiful and desirable no matter what they looked like.

Next was Tommy. Not much to say about him except he was the least likely to ever let you down. Brown hair down to the middle of his back that he usually wore in a single braid. Baby face and big brown eyes. Not much of a talker but knew just what to say when you needed a kind word. He was built a little stalky with a belly that stuck out like a pregnant woman. Not much of an athlete. More of a thinker.

Brett was raised by his father who was very strict and I used to think somewhat abusive. He took it in stride but there were times I just wanted knock that asshole out! Brett was an old soul. He was always the voice of reason....except when he was looking for a new adventure. Tommy was shorter than Brett and Sammy but not the shortest of the group.

That would be me. My name is Chris. Sporting a mediocre 5'9" body and no more than 160lbs, I looked like the youngest but was actually half a year older than the rest. I liked to keep my hair short and kind of spiked up in a messy kind of style. I am also a brown eyed shy guy with, I've heard, a dry sense of humor. I like to think I am the best dresser of the four of us. But then, I was the only one with a job and could buy my own clothes.

I can look back and remember my friends as they were then and relive that night in my mother's basement when we made plans that would change our lives forever.

It all started one Friday morning before school. It was a normal day, up at seven, quick shower; my mom had set out the box of pop tarts on the kitchen counter for my breakfast and five bucks next to it for my lunch at school as she rushed out the door to drop my sister off at school and then on to work.

She worked at a medical insurance company in the city. She had been there since I can remember. It was a good job I guess; she always said she was happy there. All I really know about it is that she looked really important with her suits and high heels every morning. She didn't talk much about what she actually did, anyway, if she did, I probably wasn't listening. She and my dad were divorced and I didn't see too much of him. He was remarried and his new wife didn't want him to have much contact with us. That never really bothered me too much.

My mom was pretty awesome. We had rules and chores but she wasn't a dictator. Sometimes she was a little overprotective but I guess that's just part of being a parent. I also have a little sister. She's four years younger than me. Her name is Camry. I know, what they were thinking, right? We got along for the most part.

We spent a lot of time on our own from early on. With only one parent and her working full time, we were what you'd call latchkey kids. There were a lot of those in Phoenix. We got out of school like an hour before Mom got off work so I would wait for my sister and we would walk home together and be alone till she came home. We had a neighbor that knew we were there and we could go to her if we had a problem and sometimes she would bring us cookies but mostly we would just watch cartoons. There were a lot of single parents in our neighborhood.

Sammy and Brett both lived on my street. They both had two parents but were also latchkey kids. Sammy had a little brother. His parents were divorced but his mom was remarried and his brother was a half-brother. His stepdad was a good guy. Sammy and his brother, Todd, were two years apart and were very different personalities but he hung out with us most of the time.

Todd was a bit heavier than the rest of us and had a thick head of curly dark brown hair. He wasn't bad looking but had an attitude like he was angry half the time. He was another one that had the girls hanging all over him. He didn't seem to like it as much as Sammy though. He was more the type to find the right girl the first time and stick with her.

We all rode bikes everywhere we went but this year we were going to be old enough to get our driver's license. I couldn't wait. I was working at the local mall at a fast food place and had been saving my money for nearly a year so I could get a down payment on a car I had my eye on.

It was a sweet 1970 Chevy Malibu two door convertible. I had saved up a thousand dollars and my mom said she would give me my half of the child support my dad sent to help me make the payments until I graduated. I hoped by then I would have it paid off. First I had to pass my driving test.

School was the same as every other Friday. I met my friends in the parking lot, had a quick smoke and made fun of the way Brett's "high and tight" made him a chick repellant.

Phoenix is great! The sun comes up too early but it's always warm and there's just something about watching that brown cloud rise up over South Mountain every morning that just lets you know, this is home.

Once the whole gang was here we headed into the gym for the Friday morning pep rally to kick off the basketball game for that night.

We watched the cheerleaders do their thing and tried not to laugh too loud at Jasmine when she missed her cue because she was trying to watch what Sammy was doing. She was for all intents and purposes, his girlfriend. Everyone knew he was never going to be faithful. She knew it too, but she was the one he called his and to her I guess that meant something.

She was pretty with her brownish red hair shimmering halfway down her back and her small hundred and five pound frame with hazel eyes that seemed to glow against her dark skin and a smile that lit up a room. She would have given the shirt off her back to help a stranger.

She was a cheerleader and hung out with the popular crowd, but she was somewhat shy and insecure. Sammy introduced her to things and people she would not normally encounter in her circles and that was exciting to her. Saturday night was date night; Friday was kind of reserved for after game parties. Jas usually hung out with her jock friends and went out with Sammy on Saturday. Sammy was happy with that arrangement. He wasn't really accepted in her crowd and that gave him a night off to pursue other interests or on occasion, hang with the guys.

This Friday was going to be what he and we all thought a fun night of getting drunk and launching things with homemade bottle rockets. Now I wish we had stuck to the plan.

For now, off to classes. One class in particular I didn't mind attending was science. I loved learning about things that could be combined and coordinated in a certain way to make almost anything the imagination could devise. Also my teacher was really cool. He had this fascination with bugs taking over the world.

That was kind of strange but he was a smart guy and always pushing our thoughts to the limit. Today was no exception. He really had a way of getting the whole class excited about learning. He taught with such dedication and enthusiasm.

I can't recall what we were learning that day but then it was six years ago. After Science class came lunch. The guys and I always grabbed a soda and bag of chips and headed out to the lawn with half the student body to catch a smoke and take in the view of South Mountain for a minute before study hall. Here we planned our weekend and what super cool things we were going to do even though all we ever really did was make plans and end up spending the weekend doing chores. Well, except for me, I had to work every weekend.

This day, however, we devised a plan that no parents or chores or job were going to keep us from. We were determined to make bottle rockets and shoot them off and have a little competition of whose would make it the highest or furthest. So it was a plan. Friday night we would catch a movie, drink a few beers, and get our bottle rockets ready for a late night launch.

After study hall, we were headed to math class when we ran into Jasmine and her annoyingly upbeat clan of snobby cheer friends. We tried to avoid them and went straight to our lockers but Jas wanted to wait for Sammy and thought the best way to run into him was to hang close to us.

She was ok, not too annoying and her friends were cute so I guess there was an upside to the situation even if they did treat us like we were slugs. She said her usual party on Friday night had been cancelled and so they were looking for something to do. She was wondering what Sammy was going to do.

Well, if Sammy wanted her to know, he would have to tell her himself. What was taking him so long? Probably hitting on some poor freshman, no doubt. Or maybe Miss Lowry, the Spanish teacher. He had no problem going after the older women either. He is such a man whore.

Thank God, here he comes down the hall with that buck tooth grin. And Jas was beaming as if that smile was for her. That was my opportunity to head on to my next class with Brett. We looked at each other as if we were both thinking the same thing.

"I hope he doesn't invite all them over tonight," Brett said. "You took the words right out of my mouth," I replied.

Just then Sammy came running up behind us. "Why did you guys take off like that? I had no way of getting out of inviting them over tonight!"

The looks on our faces could only reflect the pain and angst we felt throughout every inch of our bodies.

"This was supposed to be a night of guy stuff. Beer drinking, smoking, burping contests and danger! Chicks did not fit into that equation," Brett belted out! I'm sure Tommy and Todd wouldn't mind too much, they got along with those robots plus they were more in touch with their feminine sides than Brett and I.

Well, at least Jasmine had an older brother that would get us beer. "We'll just have to make the best of it", I replied.

I couldn't pay attention in Math class. I really like math but all I could think about was how nice it was outside and how much I didn't want to be inside.

Then all of a sudden I noticed everyone was staring at me. What the hell? Oops I guess the teacher noticed I wasn't paying attention and asked me a question. I hate it when he does that.

Mr. Hoffman was young and this was his first teaching job. He looked like a nerd and sometimes talked over our heads but he could be funny too. He was also dedicated to teaching. I remember for a while I started falling a little behind and he stayed late every afternoon until I got caught up. He really helped me a lot and never made me feel stupid for not being able to get it either.

"Sorry, Mr. Hoffman, what was the question?

Friday night at last! Mom had fixed us up with some hot wings and cheese sticks; Jasmine and her friends were getting a ride over from her brother with the beer.

Mom and Camry were going to the movies. Sammy and Todd were already here. Brett and Tommy had to finish their dinner and chores before they could come which wouldn't be too much longer. I popped "Knowing" into the DVD player and got it ready to watch.

Brett was bringing the fireworks he had left over from the 4th of July. Man, this was going to be fun.

We blasted out the tunes while we waited and played some darts. 301 was our favorite game. Sammy was pretty good but then his arms were so long he could practically touch the board when he threw with that wingspan of his.

Our house was a cookie cutter house in a fairly nice allotment. These were basement homes which they just recently started building in Phoenix. We moved into this house a year ago. Before that we lived in a townhouse not far from here. We had the basement set up as a rec room/laundry room.

It was fully equipped with TV, DVD player, and stereo, furniture we should have thrown out when we got new but instead it came down here and a bar that extended along one entire wall. Unfortunately, the bar was never stocked with anything but soda and snacks. There was also a microwave.

It can get so hot outside; sometimes this is the only place we can get cool. The dart board was on one wall and there was one brick wall with a huge picture of Einstein. I know, right. My little sister thought that as much time as I spend down here I could look at that picture and get smarter or something. Whatever.

Wow, I had almost forgotten about that picture. Wish it had made me smarter; maybe I wouldn't be sitting in this abandoned house right now. For a minute there I was so into my memories, I had almost lost the stench of the mold I was wallowing in.

Listening to the crackling fire took me back to a simpler time. A time when the worst thing I could think of was not getting that car I was saving up for.

Speaking of cars, I should have reminded them to park out back when they get here so no one sees the car in the drive.

Anyway, back to that night. I keep replaying it over and over in my mind trying to, I don't know; figure out why we went into such detail about ourselves. I guess we never thought anyone would find it, the time capsule.

It sounds so weird to even say it. "Time capsule, Time capsule." Saying it out loud feels like I'm doing something wrong and my mom just caught me. Or worse yet. The police.

It looks like the fire is dying out; I'd better gather some wood. Enough to get us through the night. As I stood up to head outside, I caught a glimpse of the full moon shining through the torn curtains. It was a full moon that night too. The night was still and there was a dense fog lying over the fields and through the woods. Nothing seemed to be stirring, it was really creepy.

As I was saying, we hadn't intended to have a party but as is turned out, there ended up more people there than we expected.

Let's see, there was me, Tommy, Sammy, Brett, Todd, Jasmine, Courtney, and Amber. Amber was kind of Todd's sometimes girlfriend. They both said they were just friends and maybe they were but it seemed sometimes like they were "friends with benefits". She was also one of Jasmine's cheer group and was very pretty with long wavy blond hair flowing down her tall slender milky white body.

She could be nice if she wanted something but a real bitch if you had nothing to offer her.

I remember hoping my mom didn't come home and get pissed thinking I planned a party knowing she would not be home. Well, she was ok with me having friends over as long as we didn't get out of hand. I just didn't tell her there would be this many kids over.

Anyway, we were being cool. We were just about to sit down to watch "Knowing" with Nicholas Cage, one of my favorite actors. Much to my surprise, even with drinking we were all glued to the TV. No one was talking, not even the girls.

My mom and Camry came home about half way through the movie and made some popcorn for us. They sat and watched the rest of it with us.

When it was over, I'm not sure who said it first; if it was Camry or one of the girls but someone shouted out, "we should make a time capsule!" Then someone else jumped on the bandwagon and it just snowballed from there. We all started getting excited about it. My mom suggested we write something about ourselves and wrap it around something we treasured.

Great idea, thanks Mom. Now we're running for our lives.

Then each of us wrote down one long synopsis about what was happening in the world today.

We commented on the gas prices, who the president was, the oil spill, the fear of global warming, and what type of music was popular.

One thing we did that they didn't do on the movie was ask questions like "what was the future like", "was time travel possible yet and if so, could we meet some day and discuss our living conditions and differences".

Who would have guessed that question would have been answered and that the future conditions had gotten to such a sad state of affairs.

Camry, being the youngest and possibly the smartest of us all, actually came up with some great ideas.
We had forgotten all about the bottle rockets and the beer if you can believe that.

She suggested we put clothes in the capsule in case they did travel back they would want to fit in with today's style. I thought it was a great idea anyway. I wouldn't want to go somewhere unknown to me and stand out like a freak.

Then Brett asked an intriguing question, since we were all different sizes, how would we know what size clothes to put in. Should we put in any women's clothes?

I don't think any of us considered it might be a woman, not even Jasmine or the other girls.

We were really getting into this and trying to leave no stone unturned. We agreed that if we put in a larger size of men's clothes, they could be belted or tied up to fit, and women wear clothes that look like men's all the time so we could put one outfit of size large men's shorts and a t-shirt in with flip flops so even a smaller foot could get around with some sort of shoe.

As I gathered wood for the fire, more and more details of that night came back to me. The longer I waited at this house alone, the more my mind drifted back to that night and I was suddenly remembering things I hadn't thought about in years.

Like, I know it's weird but I remember Amber going to pee like every twenty minutes or so. I remember thinking then that it was the beer and how glad I was that it wasn't affecting me like that for once. Now I know she was probably doing coke in the bathroom. She was a pretty girl. Too bad she never made it out of high school. They said she was all coked up with her boyfriend the night of prom when they ran off the overpass down on Black Canyon Hwy.

We lost a lot of classmates to drugs. Phoenix is a cesspool that way. Eventually the nice family oriented neighborhood we lived in became overridden with good people gone bad. Most of them ended up losing their homes though and the place is still a good place to grow up.

We all used to go all over the north side on our bikes and never felt afraid or endangered. We didn't hear too much about crime on our side of town.

With both arms full of wood, I guess it's time to head back to the house and make sure the fire hasn't gone out.

It was so dark out here that the moon and the stars looked ultra-bright and monumentally huge.

"Maybe I'll see a UFO out here." I snickered to myself. "Now I'm out here talking to myself" "I hope they get here soon."

Actually, a UFO would not surprise me in the least after what I've encountered in the last week. Phoenix can get rough but I can't imagine a place where fear of leaving your house is no longer a disease but a way of life. I guess like a lot of things, it was started with the best of intentions.

Almost to the house now. I wonder if there are as many trees in the future as there are now. Actually, I don't know if I want to know any more about the future. What is it called when you aren't told something so you can't be held responsible? Oh yes, plausible deniability. Yep, that's what I want, plausible deniability.

As I approached the house, I saw a car parked out back. The closer I get I can see that it's Tommy's car.

They've made it back. I hope they are alone and weren't followed. I laid the wood down just short of the house and crept up to the window on the side.

I had to make sure they were alone. So many things were running through my head right now. I could smell the engine was still hot and nothing was stirring. Not a breeze through the trees or any woodland animals. I had a really creepy feeling.

I poked my head up slowly until I could see into the house. I could hear talking in the distance but couldn't make out the words. I didn't recognize the voice either. I didn't see anyone.

The fire was still burning but I didn't dare go inside until I could see who was there.

Just then the back door swung open and I heard someone say, "He probably went outside to take a crap; you know how paranoid he is."

Then I heard laughter coming from the house and I knew that laugh. It was Sammy.

"Ha ha, very funny," I said as I stepped around back and confronted my longtime friends. "I was getting wood to get us through the night". "I figured we could hold up here until morning at least and could figure this thing out."

I went back to my pile of firewood and hauled it to the back of the house. It was a beautiful night. Almost reminded me of one of our camping trips.

"I hope you picked up some food while you were out", I whispered.

"Why are you whispering," Sammy shouted. "We're out here in the middle of nowhere".

He was always so fricking loud! "Keep your voice down," I scolded, "you don't know who might be looking for this guy and how far behind him they are".

"I'm not sure of anything right now", Tommy chimed in. "This is like something out of a science fiction movie." "Do you guys remember that night when we buried that thing?

Did you ever expect anything like this? I sure didn't."

"One thing is for sure, we have to find out how he got here and destroy it." Sammy added.

"Where is he?" I asked. Tommy snickered, "He's changing his clothes, I guess the stuff we buried didn't fit." Sammy belted out with a laugh, "Yeah, I seem to remember us saying make everything a large so whoever finds it can make it work, that didn't work out too good."

"Why don't we all go inside and relax", I said, "It might be a long night".

I grabbed up the wood and we all headed inside. The back door led into the kitchen.

The house was dark except for the moonlight shining in through the windows. I could see some bags on the kitchen table.

"Hope that is food," I said as I went on through to the living room, I'm starving."

"You're always starving," Tommy said, "I can't believe you're not fat as Todd." He laughed a little to himself. Then Sammy slapped him in the back of the head, "you know he had a gland problem," he said as he belted out again
with that obnoxious laugh of his. "Oh, is that it", Tommy replied, "I thought it was all those pizza's he used to eat."

Then everyone just stopped talking for a minute. "I actually miss that little punk," I said, "he was always around when we were in school but after we all left for college I guess he didn't have anyone anymore." "Yeah, Tommy added, "if I had known, I like to think I would have been there for him." "Yeah, me too," Sammy said.

We all suddenly felt very depressed thinking about the friends and in Sammy's case, family we had lost in such a short period of time.

Sammy looked at the floor and leaned against the kitchen counter and for the first time I can remember, started talking soft and low.

"Todd had gotten into a relationship with some girl from one of his classes and she introduced him to meth. That was some wicked stuff and easier to get than liquor. At first he was just getting it for her then she talked him into trying it and before any of us knew it he was hooked and my folks wanted to get help for him but he had that heart attack before they had a chance."

"Oh, man," I said as I strolled to the window so the tears wouldn't show. "I knew he had a heart attack but I thought it was from his weight or something. I didn't know any of that."

"Yeah man," added Tommy, "I'm sorry, man, I feel like crap. I should have kept in touch."

I turned around and wanted to change the subject. "Dude, where is that guy? How long does it take to change clothes?" we all walked down the hall to one of the bedrooms and peeked in.

Sitting in a window seat was Avery. He turned and looked at us as we entered the room. "Dude, what's up?" asked Sammy. "You ok? Why don't you come out here with us?" Avery started talking in a slow articulate voice. "I didn't do it, you know. I have a family."

"Ok," Sammy said, come on out here with us and we'll figure this out. "Yeah," I said, "you have to be hungry, hopefully these jug heads got some food." "You and your stomach! Yelled out Tommy, "Yes, we got food!"

Avery was an entity that has already changed our lives and was about to change the lives of everyone we came in contact with. He was the reason we were held up in this dark musty house.

Tommy and Sammy went into the kitchen to throw some grub together while Avery and I sat and stared into the fire. It wasn't cold enough for fire but it gave us enough light and killed some of the putrid stench.

"So, Avery, Who picked out your outfit?" He was wearing something that looked like it belonged on a girl. He was tall and super skinny, probably six foot four or five with spiked blond hair highlighted with blue. He was wearing cowboy boots with jean shorts and a white button-down shirt. I had to smile.

"Is that what they're wearing where you're from?" I asked. About that time Sammy and Tommy came through the door singing happy birthday with a cake full of candles in one hand and a bottle of Jack in the other. I had almost forgotten it was my birthday.

"Damn, you're all a bunch of females!" I said, "What the hell!" "You didn't think we'd forget did you, Chris?" Tommy said. Then he and Sammy started laughing. "What's so funny?" I asked. "Actually," Sammy said, "we did forget but your boy there reminded us".

"What?" I said as I shot my eyes in his direction in concerned astonishment. I guess my sudden and shocking action made him feel he needed to offer back an almost apologetic reaction.

"I have a photographic memory and remember I read the personal information you all put in your time capsule. You put your birthdate on yours." He said in a soft voice as he looked at the floor.

"Ya know, Avery, I would really like to hear more about how you came about digging that thing up, and what you're doing here. I know you said something about being from the future and fleeing from the police but there are a lot of missing details." I said as my friends looked on curiously awaiting what this stranger had to say.

About that time another car pulled into the driveway. "Holy Crap!" I yelled. Put the fire out. "We need to hide." I said as I scampered for something to douse the fire with.

Sammy ran to the window standing flush against the wall on one side and poking his head around just enough to be able to see out without being seen. Tommy and Avery fell to the floor and were attempting to belly crawl to the back door. Holding up one hand as if he were a crosswalk guard Sammy yelled, "Stop, wait, don't put out the fire!" "It's Brett and someone else I can't make out yet." "It's ok, it's Jasmine."

"Wow, haven't seen her since high school, she looks awesome!" "Sammy, you'll never change, will you?" "She probably heard you were here and wants your junk."

Tommy laughed as he picked himself up from the floor and went to the door. As he walked toward the door to greet our old friends, he and Avery dusted themselves off.

"Hey girl, glad you could make it, Brett, long time, no see. What you been up to?" Tommy said as he pushed Sammy out of the way.

"So, where's the alien?" Blurted out Brett. "He's not an alien, I said as they walked through the door, and you need to park out back. We don't want anyone passing by to see cars out here and call the police." Hey dude, happy birthday," Brett said as he handed me a bag from Radio Shack while he scoped out the room for any signs of alien activity.

"Brett, this is Avery, he claims to have come here from the future after finding our time capsule. Apparently he was looking for, well, I'll let him tell you the story now that we're all here and can get it all at once."

"First, Jas, do you mind moving the car around back while Sammy pours us all a shot of that Jack and I'll get the fire stirred." "What about the cake?" Tommy asked. "I can't believe you haven't already torn into it the way you're always whining about being hungry, Chris."

We both grinned. "Cake and Jack Daniels doesn't really sound like a gourmet dinner but I guess it'll have to do if that's all we have." I muttered to myself. Jasmine came back in from moving the car and I could hear her come in through the back door and rustle around in the cupboards and heard bags crinkling.

She entered the room with a bag of chips in one hand and a glass in the other. She made herself a drink with the coke and Jack Daniels. I guess since we were doing shots and passing around a two liter of coke, she wanted not to follow our lips on that bottle. She knew better, I laughed to myself. "What's wrong Jas?" Sammy yelled out, "You don't want to drink after us or what? You used to like swapping spit with me, remember?" We all laughed out loud.

"Yes, I remember having a crush on a jerk in high school, but thankfully you showed me what a mistake I was making when you showed up to Amber's party with Becky Jamison, *remember*?" She looked at him with her eyes opened wide and her head slightly tilted as if to say, you weren't worth it then and you're not worth it now. What a blow to Sammy's over waning ego. I had to smile at that one. I always thought Jasmine was smarter than to be one of Sammy's shadow dancers.

Now she's some kind of computer analyst or something. Brett reached up and grabbed the chips from Jasmine's hand and tore open the bag.

"What else did you find out there?" Brett asked. "I couldn't really see too much, it was pretty dark but there might have been dip." "Why didn't you grab it?" Brett complained. "Your legs broke?" Jasmine volleyed. Wow, Jasmine has really come out of her shell, I like it, I thought to myself. I scanned the room and as I stopped at Avery it appeared to me that everyone was looking at him and he was looking at the floor.

It suddenly occurred to me that we had all grown up together and trusted one another but this guy was totally out of his element and around people he didn't know but had to trust. I patted him on the shoulder, "It'll be ok, dude". I've known these guys all my life and you were lucky to find us instead of someone who might not be so trustworthy."

Then Jasmine added "that's right, Avery, I may joke about them not being there for me but since the day I met each and every one of these guys; none of them has ever not been there for me. Yes, Sammy, even you," she said as she looked at him out of the corner of her eyes with that little curl at the end of her lips.

"So, man, you were starting to tell us about why we're all here in this broken down farmhouse in the middle of nowhere," said Brett

"That's right, what's going on?" added Sammy as we all adjusted our seats and gave him our full attention.

"Well, for starters," he said, "I actually grew up over on 48th Ave and Cactus. It was an old neighborhood but still in good shape. The pollution was pretty bad then but as the years went by it got worse. In the mornings that cloud you see rising up over South Mountain was so thick you couldn't even see the thing. This air you're breathing now and the sunlight shining down are beautiful and precious.

It got so bad in the city that most of the businesses moved to the outer city, Paradise Valley and further. The government tried to clean it up but with more and more people moving here it was impossible to regulate the emissions spewing out poison. No rain except for monsoon season and every other house spitting out exhaust from meth labs, there was no way to keep it clean.

The neighborhood I lived in was like a fog laying low in the mornings and that brown cloud was no longer restricted to rising up over South Mountain, it rose up from everywhere. By the time I was in high school that neighborhood had become slums and not a good environment to raise kids so we moved further north to Gilbert.

That was about the time the government had to declare martial law so often due to violence in the city that they initiated a new form of police. There were no longer local, state and federal cops; they were all more or less hired guns."

Hey, dude, is Thrasher and still there in the future?" Brett yelled out from left field. "I used to love that place!" Brett was such a valley dude. He loved skateboarding and that was the best activities park in the whole state. Skateboarders, motocross, dune surfing, the best extreme athletes practiced there.

Avery looked at him like what? Thrasher what? We all knew how Brett was and just ignored him. "Anyway, go on with your story and ignore him," I said. "We all do." Everyone laughed for a minute, even Brett who grabbed another log and put it on the fire as he made his way to the kitchen.

"Anyway", Avery resumed in his soft spoken voice, "like I said we moved to Gilbert and there I had one year left of high school and was already accepted to Arizona State on a Baseball scholarship. I met this girl, Temper. She was beautiful and we were making plans to get out of the pollution and find a place outside the city where we and hopefully our kids one day could actually go outside without the worry of Valley Fever or a hundred other diseases floating around in that cloud.

At that moment you could almost feel the pain in his heart and we didn't even know what was yet to come from the stranger's mouth.

I looked at Jasmine and she had a look on her face like she was thinking the same as me. Then he continued "It was a wonderful day when Temper was also accepted to ASU. We celebrated that night by going to dinner at The Point."

"You mean the place on Pinnacle Peak?" Asked Jasmine, "I love that place. I'm happy to hear that it's still there. Sammy and I used to sneak up there at night and use the hot tub at the hotel.

Remember that Sammy," she asked as she looked at him this time with a gleam in her eye. He looked at her with a soft smile that I for one had never seen on his face before. He glanced down at the floor and then back up at her and it seemed as though they were sharing a moment of sweet memories. "What year was that?" Jasmine asked the stranger.

"That was a great question. How far into the future are we talking about?" I asked as everyone sat up a little in their seats. "Where's that dip you were talking about, Jas?" Brett asked as he came out of the kitchen. "Wait a minute, did I just walk in on you guys talking about me? Why is everyone looking at me?"

"Oh my gosh," Tommy gasped, "You have the worst timing!" No, no one was talking about you. We are trying to listen to Avery's story and find out what the hell is going on here. Sit down and shut up and forget about that stupid dip!" "Damn you're annoying sometimes!"

Avery, please give me a minute to find this guy some dip for his chips before he has a meltdown. I'll be right back," Jasmine said as she got up to retrieve the dip for Brett. "I have to use the little girl's room anyway." Avery smiled at her as she walked out of the room.

"Well, let's fill up these shot glasses while we're waiting and I need to take a piss too" said Tommy. "I'll just step outside though. Anyone else have to go?" With that invitation, all of us stepped out back to take care of business. "Maybe we should all grab some more wood while we're out here. Looks like we're getting low in there." I finished up about the same time as Avery so we headed into the woods to look for some logs worthy of our fire. We had no tools to cut so it was hard to find anything worth keeping that was not too long.

"Have things changed so much in the future?" I asked Avery. "Well, there are places that have changed very little, places that have changed for the better and places that have deteriorated to a point that they have been abandoned. Mostly people are the same. The government is restructured and unrecognizable from your present political structure. I guess I should have thought to bring some history books back with me."

I didn't hear Sammy walking up behind us until he chimed in with, "At least there's still baseball, right, you said you were a baseball player for ASU, yeah, go Sun Devils!"

"I said I had a scholarship for baseball, that was a long time ago and before the assassinations started." Said Avery as he walked off by himself with an armload of wood. Sammy and I looked at each other with our eyebrows perched high on our foreheads. "Assassinations?" "Is that what he said?" I shouted as I headed back towards the house with Sammy leaving our strange new friend in the distance looking up at the stars as if he were silently speaking to God.

Brett came running up behind us, no wood, grabbed us both by the back of the neck and whispered, "look at him talking to the stars, I told you he was an alien." We all laughed and looked up as if we were expecting to see something. Then looked at each other and laughed again.

We brought our meager offerings of wood and piled them up outside the back door at the bottom of the stairs.

As we entered the house one by one, Jasmine was standing in the kitchen with a photo album in one hand and a jar of dip in the other.

"Here's your dip" she said as she handed the bottle to Brett with a little cock of her head "and here's something else that might interest you three" she said as she held up the photo album index finger extended pointing at one of the photos.

It was too dark to make out the contents of the photo so we went into the living room. Jas ducked a little to see out the window looking for Avery.

"Chris, this is really creeping me out. Look closely at this picture; it is definitely Avery but look closer at the background. He's standing in front of this house! This house", she repeated. Then I could see that she was so frightened by the thought of the implications of everything she was crying.

"LOOK!" She shouted at us. "That must be Temper and their baby! I'm so scared, I want to leave. We're out here in the middle of nowhere and no one knows we're here.

This is how horror movies start. We know nothing about this guy and you have to admit that his story sounds really far-fetched. He could have lured us here to kill us! Don't you guys get it! This was or is his house! He might have..."

Just then Avery walked into the living room. "Killed my family here? Is that what you were about to say?"

I felt a lump in my throat as I grabbed Jasmine's hand not taking my eyes off him. Tommy walked in behind Avery and as he turned to look at him Sammy and Brett tackled Avery to the ground.

"What the hell!" shouted Tommy "Give me that fricken bottle! You all are crazy!" "No," Jasmine said, "this is a photo album I found in the kitchen and this guy used to live here with his wife and kid. Now they're missing.

We need to get the hell out of here and call the police!" Sammy had Avery in a choke hold while Brett looked around for something to tie him up with. "This is crazy", said Tommy. "Let him go! He's not lying!" "You're as crazy as him" yelled Chris as Jasmine started to shake and held on for dear life.

"There's no such thing as time travel. This nutcase dug up our time capsule and we were stupid enough to believe him." "Stop", Tommy said in a low, calm voice. "Let him go, Sammy. Everyone just calm down. I saw it." At that moment, everyone stopped dead in their tracks and all eyes were on Tommy. "That's right, I saw the time machine. I actually made him prove it to me and I traveled back a couple years."

"Shut the hell up!" Brett interrupted; "This asshole gave you some kind of drugs. He's crazy, isn't he? Chris? This can't be true. How can this be his house and its old now, it would be torn down by his time. I'm so... This is unreal...Where the hell is that bottle?"

Brett grabbed the bottle of Jack from the table and sat down on the sheet covered couch shaking his head back and forth as he tipped back the bottle and took a huge swig then stared at the floor. We all took seats slowly as the stranger and Tommy continued with the most unbelievable story we could ever imagine.

"I didn't murder my family," Avery said in a soft, calm voice. "When we found out that Temper was pregnant, we were determined to get out of the life we had been thrown into.

There had been talk of research on time travel and I offered myself as an apprentice to the work under a brilliant scientist that you may recognize by the name, Albert Einstein. I know what you're all thinking. Albert Einstein is dead.

Are you sure about that? He had started his research in the time of the Second World War and was recruited by Hitler to build a device for him to travel into the future to get information on technologies not yet developed.

Are you all familiar with the works of Einstein? Well, in 1916 he had just recently became a German citizen and was the Director of the Kaiser Wilhelm Physical Institute and Professor in the University of Berlin.

Here he realized the inadequacies of Newtonian mechanics and his special theory of relativity stemmed from an attempt to reconcile the laws of mechanics with the laws of the electromagnetic field.

It was here that he developed the photon theory of light and in 1916 when he published his paper on the general theory of relativity; he also tried to publish theories on the effect of quantum monatomic gas and the atomic transition probabilities and relativistic cosmology which enabled time travel."

I looked around the room and saw Brett looking into his bottle of whiskey, Jasmine pulling fuzz from her sweater and Chris really getting into a full meal of nail biting and I knew he was losing them so I banged my fist down on the coffee table and yelled out,"

"Guys! I know this is over our heads but you have to pay attention!" "Our lives may depend on you listening and listening well to what this man is telling you."

"Tommy," Chris said with a halfcocked snicker, "I can listen all day but without some kind of proof, I just can't believe any of this. Albert Einstein, alive? Come on, you're asking us to forget everything we've been taught all our lives and our parents before us on the word of someone we just met!"

"That's right", Jasmine added "This is a lot to take in without a shred of evidence."

"Evidence!" Avery said in a slightly louder and more abrupt voice than he had used up to now. "Look around you, does this house look like the one in that picture? No, it looks like it did in 1985 when we moved into it yet I look the same as I do now. Does that say anything to you?"

"If you don't want to help me, fine but now that you have heard my story, if you try to tell anyone out there the secret police could hear about it and where my house is and that could jeopardize my being able to find my wife and daughter and I can't let that happen!"

With that, Chris and Brett both quickly rose to their feet in a defensive irritated frenzy while Sammy looked on in fear and anger that now this was getting threatening and out of hand.

"Whoa, Whoa" Tommy shouted as he rose to his feet to defend Avery. "You all trust me, right?"

"Did I not say that I saw the time machine? That I traveled back in time in it? He's telling you the truth and I for one want to know more. I know it sounds crazy and scary, but we are in this now and we're going to see it through."

"I want to see it", Jasmine squeaked out from behind Chris. "I need to know that this is for real before I listen to any more theories of Einstein."

"I promise", said Tommy, "Everyone just sit down and let him finish and everyone will see it." With that, Brett and Chris sat down and Chris motioned to Brett to give him the bottle. Brett handed it over as Sammy put his hand out to get it next and Jasmine looked into her nearly finished glass and sat it down on the end table.

Tommy looked at Avery and asked him to continue.

"As you know, Hitler had another use for Einstein's ideas and so he moved to America and took up residency here hoping to develop his time machine without lending it to the evil he saw before him in Germany.
By the 1920's, he constructed his unified field theories which included a theory on gravitation. Once he perfected his machine, he embarked on his journey into the future where he was free to work on his ideas without government involvement."

"He faked his death in 1955 and I met him in 2115 under the name Yancy Schmitt. Hard to believe, isn't it. Well, I assure you it is all true and his theories work, however, even in our time, they are not accepted nor are they marketed. This is only known by Yancy, my wife and I."

"Jasmine, you found that picture album and figured out that this is my house. You are right, with Yancy's help, my family and I came back in time and lived here for years.

We were happy here until something started happening to our child. She didn't transport as well as we did. Her undeveloped body could not handle the stress that time travel takes on you and as she grew; this became more apparent and we were afraid we were going to lose her.

We, against Yancy's warnings, made another leap back into the future to try and find him for help. When we tried to return, there were complications and my wife and daughter became separated from me somewhere in time.

To me it had been years but to everyone else in our time it had only been a month.

I returned to find Temper's family had the police looking for me and they were accusing me of murder and trying to hide from what I had done.

When I attempted to contact Yance, the police were waiting on me. I hid in an abandoned house on the north side which I assume was Chris' house because that's where I stumbled upon the time capsule."

"So, wait a minute," said Sammy, "you came here back in time with your wife and baby and lived here for how many years? Then your kid got sick so you went back to the place you fled from but only you made it. Am I right so far? Then you saw the cops were after you and again you and only you accurately made it back." Is that the short and skinny? Because I'm kinda thinkin like those other folks in the future; How come you can zip back and forth but your wife and kid got lost? Also, Tommy, you said you accurately went two years ahead and right back with no problem, right?"

"Anyone else see this as weird?"

"Yea, you make a really good point, Sammy". Jas chimed in. "Tommy? What's up with that?" she continued." Why were his wife and kid the only ones to not make it?" With that, all eyes were on Tommy and Avery waiting for some kind of answer that would take away the fear that he still could be a murderer.

The fire started going out. Everyone had been so engrossed in the talk of the time machine; no one was paying attention to the fire."

Chris stopped biting his nails for a minute and broke the silence with "Looks like we need some more wood for the fire."

"Yea, anyone need anything from the kitchen?" Brett stated as he stood and looked toward the kitchen doorway. He ran his fingers through his hair and blew out a huge sigh as if to say this was all becoming too unbelievable. Then with one giant step he headed toward the door.

Avery looked at Tommy and raised his eyebrows. "I don't know what to say or do to make them understand that even though we made it, the sheer physics of this is still experimental and there are kinks that we don't yet understand and without Yance I don't know if I can figure it out."

I saw tears fill up in the wells of his eyes and in my heart, I felt he was not a killer and that he was determined to do whatever it would take to find his family.

"I felt so alone and helpless until I found that time capsule and read all your descriptions. I was convinced that I had found a tribe of good and kind people to help me. The thing is, the secret police could and probably would force Yance to give them his findings and they would have the capability to make their own time travel source.

I also believe they would have to kill him to get it. I need to find my family before they have the ability to travel through time and hunt me down."

Jasmine stood and stretched as she threw her hair back behind her shoulder, "I need to use the little girl's room again." "Brett," she shouted into the kitchen, "would you please cut me a piece of that cake? I have a feeling this is going to be a long night."

"Sure thing sweetheart", Brett yelled back in his Bogie voice.

"Um, I'm really sorry to ask this", Tommy said as he stood up from the arm of the couch he had been sitting on, "But could you leave me your cell phone, please?"

Jasmine's mouth dropped open about an inch as she looked at Tommy with confusion and annoyance. "You want my cell phone? Is that what you said? Since when has there been a trust issue between us?" She said.

"Who are you and where is my friend Tommy that I've known all my life?" She reached into her pocket and pulled out her phone and slammed it down into Tommy's hand in anger and dismay at how her friend was taking the side of a stranger over his friends.

She bolted down the hallway muttering to herself as she slammed the bathroom door.

Chris stood up and reached into his pocket and pulled out his phone too and slammed it down onto the coffee table as he looked at Tommy and Avery and said in a low and disapproving voice, "I'm gonna go help Brett in the kitchen and get some wood."

He walked toward the kitchen door and turned back to look at Sammy as he disappeared through the doorway. Sammy set down the bottle of Jack Daniels he was coddling and stood up.

With a long stretch, he exclaimed, "Well, I guess that's my cue." "I'm gonna go see what my friends are up to." He said with emphasis on friends as if Tommy were no longer one.

As he exited the living room, he turned to Tommy and Avery and said with his classic snicker, "Don't worry, I don't have my phone on me." then he disappeared into the darkness of the kitchen.

Avery looked at Tommy and they both smiled at each other as if they were both thinking the same thing. "I think it's time to show them", said Avery. "You took the words right out of my mouth", replied Tommy. They both stood and Tommy called to Jasmine to come outside when she finished in the bathroom. Tommy and Avery followed their friends outside to the woodpile and waited on Jas to join them.

Arizona nights are so nice. Being so far from the city, the stars look so big and there are so many. A warm breeze blew through the trees. The moon seemed larger than ever and the smell of grapefruit filled the air from the grove next door. As Jasmine walked out the door and down the stairs, you could see she was not happy to be there and the joy of seeing her friends once again had turned to fear of never seeing tomorrow.

"So," said Tommy, "I guess you know why we asked all of you to come out here."

"It's time to let you in on something that I have trusted no one with except my wife and Tommy" Avery butted in. "I trust you all now because I believe in your strong bond as friends and that you will take this information in the strictest confidence and not run with it like a thief in the night and use it for capital gain. I know in this century with money being a major issue that would be very tempting."

You could hear total silence at that moment, not a creature stirring in the woods, no breeze blowing in the trees. No one took a breath as all eyes and ears were glued to Avery awaiting his secret to time travel.

Avery reached into his pocket and pulled out a little box that looked a lot like a universal remote control to an old television. He looked at it with extreme intensity. Sammy of course was the first to break the silence.

"Oh, what the," he laughed out loud with his mouth open wide and his head tilted back as he grabbed his head and clinched his hair. "A remote control! Dude! What is this?"

His voice became increasingly irritated. And his face was no longer laughing.

Oh, man! Jasmine grabbed Sammy's arm and looked closer at the object in Avery's hand as Avery looked at everyone as if they were the one's not being serious. "Sammy, would you like to give me a ride home?" Jasmine asked. "I knew this guy was crazy and we were just as crazy to even listen. Tommy, really? Nice to see everyone again, next time though, can we just have lunch? Happy Birthday, Chris." She gave a tug to Sammy as if to initiate the departure.

Brett, shoving cake into his mouth laughed out spitting cake crumbs all over himself. "Man, you really had us going, Tommy", he said. Then Brett headed for the woodpile to get more wood for the fire. "We gonna stay here tonight? It can still be fun like when we used to camp out only in a really old house. Chris, buddy? It's your birthday, what do you want to do?" asked Brett.

Before Chris could answer and before Sammy and Jasmine could walk away, Avery closed his eyes and as if in slow motion, everything around us seemed to get blurry and change colors and then everything went black for a split second. Within less than a minute, colors were visible again and the sun was shining and we were no longer standing outside that old abandoned shack but at Chris' house where we buried the time capsule. We could hear Camry inside talking on the phone.

"I think I'm going to be sick", said Jasmine. "Seriously, I feel like I'm going to throw up!"

Just then, Brett did throw up and Chris was blowing his cheeks out trying not to. "It's one of the side effects," Tommy said as he raised his fist to his mouth. "It won't last long," he added as he held back a burp.

"I can hear Camry on the phone", sputtered Chris as he held his stomach.

"It wouldn't be a good idea to let her see us." He no more got the words out of his mouth when she came out on the patio and yelled out to them.

She quickly got off the phone and started toward us. "Mom," she yelled toward the house, when did Chris get home?" We all ran toward her trying to shut her up, but the next thing we knew, we were back in the blackness again and then the abandoned house started to reappear. Apparently, Avery panicked and sent us back to where we started.

"What just happened?" Jasmine yelled out as she started to run behind the stairs to the house to vomit.

"Dude!" Belted out Brett as he grabbed his stomach. "What was that?" Did we just do what I think we did?" He put one hand on his knee in an attempt to control his queasiness and the other hand out in front of him waving it in front of Avery. "Drop the remote! Drop that mother fucker right fuckin now!"

Sammy lay down on the ground staring into space. "Oh my God! Oh my God." Was all he could get out.

Jas sat down on the bottom step with her head between her legs, Chris sat on the wood pile staring in amazement at Tommy and Tommy stood next to Avery grinning from ear to ear.

"That's the time machine? " Asked Chris. "I was expecting some sort of vehicle like on "Back_to the Future" or the movie "Time Machine" not some little TV remote!"

"It's a device that Yance developed to, you might say, harness and control a natural energy singularity or black hole that bends time so you can simply walk through the folds into another place and time.

This is where my wife and daughter became separated. When you bend something there is a point at the fold where there are pockets and in this case it's my theory that they went through at a pocket while I went straight through.

If I am right and I believe I am, they not only went into a time change but a geographical change which means they could be anywhere on this planet."

"Well, hell, maybe they're on another planet," Sammy ripped out with sarcasm.

Chris kicked him and scolded him for that inappropriate outburst. "That's not even funny, dude." "This just got too fricken real for me. I don't know what you expect us to do to help you. You're talking quantum physics and we're still trying to grasp chemistry. We don't know, well, I don't know anything about shit like that."

"Yea, Brett finally settled his stomach down and chimed in. "You would think with the brain power of Albert Einstein, you two would have come up with some failsafe option that would track every leap and you could pull it up on a computer or something like runners do with their GPS navigators they wear."

"That would be great but it probably wouldn't pick up outside the satellite systems. The GPS locates from satellites, Brett." Avery explained.

"Oh, yea, I see your point," said Brett. "But there should be something like a redial, I don't know. All I know is that if you can't find your family what makes you think the police from your time can find you?"

"They can access the information from Yance's transmissions if they gain the device. The reason I can't find my family is because there was no intended destination. Let's say you and Sammy told Chris you were going to take the bus from Phoenix to Glendale but somewhere along the route, Sammy saw a girl and jumped off the bus say at 7th street. Later when you reached Glendale you called Chris and he asked where Sammy was.

You would have no idea. If he never resurfaced, who do you think would be the prime suspect? You right? It would be your word alone to prove he jumped off the bus; where you however, could be easily traced to the end of your stop. That's sort of the way this happened only more dimensional."

"I know my house doesn't look like much right now but it still has four bedrooms and hopefully no unwanted guests; so I suggest we all pick a room and get some sleep. We really need to get an early start in the morning and it's already 2am." Said Avery.

"I don't know if I can sleep after everything that's happened" said Tommy.

"Spend the night?" Jasmine yelled out in horror. "I can't stay all night; I have stuff to do tomorrow. I thought we were coming here to celebrate Chris' birthday. I don't have a change of clothes or anything."

"Well", said Sammy with an evil grin on his face, "If you're worried about wearing wrinkled clothes tomorrow, you can always stay in my room and sleep naked and I can keep watch so no one tries anything with you."

Then he laughed out loud like he was trying to play it off like a joke but we all smiled knowing if he could get away with it he would. Jasmine just looked at him with her head tilted to the side as if to say thanks but not in your wildest dreams.

"None of us brought things for a stay over, Jas." Said Tommy. "You are free to leave if you want, any of you can leave right now but this is the discovery of a lifetime and I for one do not want to let this guy or that remote as you call it out of my sight. Not to mention, he came to us for help."

Brett grabbed Jasmine's hand and led her into the house. He assured her if she stayed and saw this thing through with the rest of them, it could change her life and all of their lives.

She listened while he actually talked to her like an intelligent human being for once. It almost gave her chills. He was so intense in his argument that she decided she would at least attempt to see it through but if it got weird, I mean weirder, or dangerous, she was bugging out.

He got the large tank top out of the time capsule and gave it to her to wear to sleep in. "This is the best I can do, sweetheart" Brett said in his Bogie imitation that he liked to use.

She reluctantly accepted it and found a room upstairs. Shortly after she was out of sight, the rest of the gang followed her upstairs with Brett and Tommy sharing a room and Chris and Sammy sharing and Avery sleeping in his own master bedroom.

There was no electricity so the only light coming in was from the moon and stars. No one talked but I really don't think anyone slept either. Every tumbleweed that blew down the road sounded like a mac truck and the wind blowing through the trees gave the illusion of voices in the distance. No, I really don't think anyone slept that night.

Chapter 2

The Journey Begins

The next morning as we all made our way back down the stairs to the living room we were not surprised to hear Jasmine in the kitchen serving up a very much appreciated breakfast of egg McMuffins and OJ from the nearby McDonalds. Sammy was the first to break the silence. Mmmmmm, something smells good as he made his way around the hallway into the kitchen.

"You need any help?" He asked as Jasmine looked around for plates.

"Sure," she said as she smiled at him perhaps imagining, wondering if this is what it would have been like if they would have stayed together.

"See if there's any ketchup in the pantry. They forgot to put it in the bag for the hash browns." "Now there's a surprise." Replied Sammy as they both giggled a little.

"Well, there's an unopened bottle here but the expiration is 1989. You think it's still good? They both laughed as they shook their heads and Jasmine commented "Better not chance it. Just help me take these into the dining room. At least we can eat like civilized people."

The house was well lit now with the sun shining into every room and the dining room was overlooked in the darkness the night before. It was separated from the kitchen by French doors that opened into a wonderful room almost like an Arizona room but enclosed with wall and windows as opposed to all window. The furniture was covered with sheets so Sammy called for more help. "You all want to eat you need to come in here and clear off some of this furniture!"

As they entered the kitchen one by one all were surprised to see this room that was undetected the night before. It was like something out of an episode of Cribs. Antique cherry wood china cabinets filled with the most delicate and beautiful china they had ever seen and the hint of pale sea green walls were almost magical in the shimmering of the morning sun.

The large windows had stained glass border that made color dance across the eight place setting dining table. There was an antique cherry wood buffet with a handmade delicate doily under a beautiful lamp of pewter and sea green vase base with a lampshade that complimented the décor as if it were made for the room.

Avery was the last to enter the room. He rubbed his head and stretched grabbing the entrance with both arms extended. "This is my wife's favorite room." He said.

"She pondered over every detail for weeks before making a decision. Most of the furniture she picked up in estate sales and refinished herself. She's really good at decorating" he said as he lowered his head rubbing his hand across the grain of the dining room table.

We all remained silent for a moment as we took our seats.

As we ate, we took turns telling stories about remember when. From time to time I glanced up at Avery and although he smiled at some of the stories, I could see he was anxious to get started but not even sure himself how.

Suddenly everyone became silent and looked at each other. "What was that?" Said Chris. "I heard it too" said Tommy. "You guys are paranoid and hearing things" mocked Brett.

"There it was again! That definitely sounded like a car door." shouted Chris. We all looked at each other, then at Avery. Everyone jumped up at the same time to run to the window. From where we were, we couldn't see the cars nor did we see anything else.

We heard footsteps coming up the stairs at the back door. We didn't know if we should see who it is or hide. We all seemed to be frozen in place unable to speak or move. Jasmine raised her hand over her mouth as her eyes grew wider staring at the French doors that led to the kitchen. Sammy stepped in front of her and she grabbed his arm so as not to be left behind should we run for it. Avery held his arm up motioning us to back up as he cautiously made his way to the edge of the doors looking into the kitchen. The next thing we all knew, we were standing in front of the Metrocenter Mall in town feeling queasy and disoriented.

"What the fuck!" Spewed out Brett with a little vomit. Sammy wrapped his arms around Jasmine and asked her if she was ok.

"I think so, what just happened?" She asked already knowing the answer. People were walking by looking at us as if we were drunken teenagers. That's exactly what we felt like.

"Dude! You have to give us some warning before you do that shit!" Exclaimed Chris who was bent over holding his knees trying to keep from hurling.

"What happened man?" Tommy asked Avery. "What the fuck did you see? Who was at the house?" He grabbed Avery by the shirt and pulled his face close. "What the fuck did you see?"

Avery knocked Tommy's hands loose from his shirt as all eyes were on him awaiting an explanation. His eyes opened wide as he pushed Tommy toward the entrance to the Mall and told us all to get inside. The urgency in his voice told us not to argue or ask questions, just get inside as quickly as possible.

When we got there we saw a very unfamiliar place. This mall was where we did most of our shopping but nothing looked the same.

As we all slowly walked around in circles amazed at the design and colors of an otherwise commonplace and dreary collaboration of mediocre storefronts we saw stores we'd never heard of with clothes designs we never saw before.

Bazaar videos showing on billboard flat screens everywhere. We were so distracted we didn't see what happened to Avery.

We tried to pull it together and act normal but we were totally out of our comfort zone. It was obvious we weren't dressed like anyone else and people were starting to stare.

Tommy looked himself up and down, and then looked at all of us. "What year do you think this is?" He asked. "We need to find some clothes and a place to change before we draw any more attention to ourselves."

"Where the hell is Avery?" Jasmine asked as she took Sammy's hand and sort of used him as a human shield to hide her unusual appearance. He put his arm around her and told her to act casual and they would think she was sporting a new retro style.

Everyone laughed but still felt uncomfortable as they walked through the mall looking for a store that might have clothes. And one eye peeled looking for Avery.

"Dude, how could he abandon us like this not knowing anything about this time?" Said Brett. "This is messed up".

"I'm sure he's around here somewhere." Said Tommy, "We just got separated. He's probably looking for us too."

"What if he went through one of those fold corners like he said his wife did?" Asked Chris, "We could be stuck here forever. He has the remote!"

"You're a bonehead" laughed Brett, "We were with him when we landed. We all came here together." Brett laughed even harder when he saw the look on Chris' face like he was trying to sort it all out in his head.

"Yea, that's right" he answered after like three minutes of pondering.

"Look at him;" said Sammy, "He still looks like he doesn't get it." Then everyone laughed except Tommy who just smiled and put his hand on Chris' shoulder. "Don't worry about it man. Avery is here somewhere."

We finally found a clothing store and went inside. The styles were jacked up kind of like skater on steroids.

"I wonder if there is a store that sells adult clothes" said Chris who was always the style conscious one. He no more than got the words out of his mouth when we heard a voice come from behind us saying, "May I help you?"

We all turned around and Chris blurted out, "I was just wondering if you sell or know where we can buy a more adult style of clothes." We all looked on as the store clerk directed us to a back room where we thought we were going to find more clothes; instead there was Avery sitting at a table smiling from ear to ear.

"Bout time you made it in here. Anyone hungry?" "What the Hell, Avery?" Yelled Sammy, "What the fuck are you smiling about? What are we doing here and why did you take off like that?"

"Not cool, Dude." Interjected Brett as he leaned on the back of a chair. Tommy just looked at him shaking his head.

"Man, if you can bump in and out of time like this whenever you see whatever it was you saw, why do you need us? Just take us back to our own time and leave us alone. This is not a game that any of us asked to play."

Avery slammed his fist down on the table in front of him. This is not a game to me either! My wife and daughter are out there lost and I do need your help to find them and find them in your time. You need to trust me that we had to get out of there and in a hurry.

There were police from your time coming through the door. I know they were from your time otherwise we would never have seen or heard them coming!"

"This is my time and we can't stay here long. Now everyone please sit down, calm down, and have something to eat while we have a safe place to plan our next move. We can stay here for maybe an hour or two while I try to contact Yancy. We can trust everyone here but trust no one else! Probably best if you don't wander around too much either, you all stick out like a sore thumb here and there are cameras everywhere. I sent for some Chinese to be delivered so I hope you all like it."

"I'm starving" said Chris and "I love Chinese!"

Everyone just looked around at each other and smiled waiting for someone to say it and sure enough Brett could never hold his tongue. With a snicker in his voice he said, "Really?" Which was enough said since we all knew that Chris was perpetually hungry and we all laughed halfheartedly. Even Brett would have a hard time distracting us from this fear and angst we were feeling. Maybe Chris had an iron clad stomach but I don't think the rest of us were thinking about food.

"How can you eat," said Jasmine, "My whole body is like quaking internally. Not to mention, I think I'm still queasy from that leap."

When she said that; Avery looked at her like he wanted to jump across the table and put his hand over her mouth. He looked at her, then at his friend that directed us to the back room.

His friend didn't seem to notice or didn't react in any way but it was clear that he didn't know the whole story and we needed to be more discreet.

We all took a seat at the table while Avery and his friend stepped into another room. We all looked at Jasmine then at each other.

"Is it me or does everyone feel creeped out here?" Asked Jasmine. "I'm guessing this friend of his doesn't know where we're from by the look on Avery's face after Jas made that leap comment," said Sammy.

"I know, right?" Said Brett, "I thought he was going to leap across the table and knock her out." He chuckled a little. "Get it, leap across the table, leap, and...... never mind." He rolled his eyes up as he glanced around the room to avoid eye contact after that poor excuse for a joke he was fumbling with.

"When's the food going to get here?" said Chris.

"I don't know about you guys but I'd like to see what my house looks like now," said Tommy, always curious. "Anyone up for a little sightseeing?" "Dude! I don't want to leave this room!" exclaimed Sammy.

"That's sounds like a good idea" said Avery as he walked into the room with the food. Jasmine and Sammy looked at each other as if they were communicating telepathically while Tommy looked at the table and Brett looked at Tommy.

Chris of course started digging in to the Chinese. There was enough to feed a small army. Avery took his place at the head of the table and started passing around the food cartons with chopsticks and paper plates.

No one spoke as they dished up a portion of each carton to their plates. Chris was chowing while everyone else was just pushing their rice and hibachi chicken around with their chopsticks.

"This is really good" Chris literally spit out as he spoke with his mouth full of the train wreck he was chewing. "Isn't anyone else eating?" He paused from his gorge for a moment to take notice.

That must have been a cue to open the floodgate, everyone started to talk at the same time. Brett with his wit asking if this was the last supper and Jasmine wanting a complete account of what was expected of us and Tommy and Sammy both wanting to know more about the future since they were in it.

Avery just sat patiently waiting for the outburst to wind down before speaking. "I had to get us out of there. Did any of you want to answer questions about why you were breaking into an abandoned house?

Plus, it gave me an opportunity to try to make contact with Yancy. While my friend went for the food he went by Yancy's shop but no one was there. I tried to contact him at his house but no luck.

His Holibot said he was being detained so it looks like the Marshals will be on my trail by now. We need to get back to your time and then things are going to get a little crazy.

The Marshals don't know anything about your time or your time capsule. That should buy me a little time. They can't get that information from Yancy because I never got a chance to tell him about it.

Now, where would be the best place to leap back to? I'm thinking that if we leap back to the night before at my house we could bug out before your local cops show up. Any ideas where we could go from there? I don't want to go too far because with my house being the last place I was with them, that would most likely be the place to reenact the leap and possibly I can step into the same fold and end up with my family. Just a theory.

I only need you to help me hide until I make that leap. If I'm successful, you'll never have to see me again. If not..." Avery looked down at his plate of uneaten food and shook his head. In a quiet and almost sobbing voice he said, I know none of you asked to share in my troubles and I am sorry for this but my life has no meaning if I can't find my family."

Everyone just sat there in silence for a second or two as Avery's words sunk deep into their souls; thinking about their own families and to what lengths they would go through to find them if the roles were reversed.

Tommy looked up at Avery who was still bowing into his dish of untouched chicken on the table. As he rested his hand on Avery's shoulder he grabbed the hand of Jasmine who was seated to his right and she grabbed the hand of Sammy as she looked deep into his eyes as if to say we are all family here and need to stick together.

Sammy looked at Brett sitting at the end of the table and gave a halfcocked smile. Brett responded with an even bigger smile as he said. "Dude, I get it, but you're not gonna hold my hand." Everyone laughed and Tommy looked at Chris and said, "Remember when we were getting ready to leave for college and I was so bummed out about leaving my family and friends? Do you remember what you told me?"

Chris nodded his head in a matter of fact motion and said. "Sure do, I told you not to be bummed out, they will be right where you left them when you get back and if not you would always have us." With that everyone looked at Avery and Tommy still holding on to his shoulder said, "I think I speak for all of us when I say we can appreciate how you feel and will do whatever we can to help you find your family and if not you'll always have us.

Jasmine wiping the tears that had welled up in her eyes leaned toward Sammy and kissed him; then scanning the rest of the group she expressed how much she loved every one of them and would do what she could to help out.

"How about this Chinese," Brett busted out to break up the solemn mood. Everyone took a deep breath wiped their eyes and started to eat. Avery sat at the end of the table admiring his new friends and really felt a bond building with this very special group he had stumbled upon.

"Hey, I just thought of something," Chris said grinning from ear to ear. "If we go back to the night before, it'll be my birthday all over again." "Maybe this time instead of a bottle of Jack, I can get one of those remotes. That would be an awesome birthday gift!" Even Avery had to smile at that one.

"I have a question", said Jasmine. "I was just wondering, if every time we leap we run the risk of catching one of those folds, shouldn't we just go back to exactly when we came from and not leap anymore? I mean, I kinda like being twenty four and I really like my life right now. I don't want to be lost and alone. Sorry Avery."

"No, Jas, you're right and my wife and I had almost decided to get rid of the device when our daughter got worse and we knew the medicine of the time would not be able to help her. Believe me guys; I don't want to lose anyone else. As soon as my friend gets back, we'll be returning to 2014."

"What are you doing? I mean, what are we waiting for?" Asked Sammy as all eyes turned to Avery. "You said we could only stay for an hour or two and it's had to be that long if not longer." "We could have looked up where we used to live by now, maybe looked in the library or a computer somewhere to see if we ever had kids, maybe see if I ever did anything with my life."

"That's exactly why I had you all brought in here so you wouldn't wander around and try to find information on your future. That could change the outcome of all that was to be. Just like you can't travel back within your lifetime, to many things could become altered."

Everyone just looked around kind of speechless. "Dang, said Brett, "There are a lot of things we need to learn about this time travel stuff.

Now I know why everyone doesn't have one of those little gizmos. You have to be a rocket scientist to know how to use it." "I think when we get back to our time, I want to go see my family before we do anything else just in case things don't work out the way we want," Chris said as he looked at Jasmine who was hanging on tightly to Sammy's arm.

She looked back and for a second I almost thought I saw her say with her expression, "If we get back". Then I looked at Brett who was sucking up a noodle shaking his head up and down. And once again a feeling of utter anxiety and fear seemed to fill the room. Goosebumps engulfed my body.

"It's taking him way too long." Said Avery with much concern in his voice. "Maybe we should move out into the open for a minute to get a feel for anything unusual. You guys should probably grab a change of clothes so you don't stand out."

With that Jasmine's eyes lit up. That was the first time I'd seen her smile since this whole ordeal began. "She has such a beautiful smile", thought Chris.

"Hahaha" laughed Brett out loud, "Look at Jasmines face. It's funny how quickly a girl forgets her life's in danger when you mention the word shopping."

"I wouldn't mind a little fashion gazing myself," Said Chris. "I swear you're gay!" Said Sammy. They all laughed but no one really knew. Chris was style conscious and no one had ever seen him with a girl. I guess we just accepted him the way he was and never gave it a thought. Chris was just Chris.

"I think maybe we should split up and go out in pairs so as not to be so conspicuous. Once you get your clothes, come straight back here. Tommy, you and I will team up, and the rest of you choose a partner. We will meet back here in half an hour.

"What do we use for money?" Asked Sammy. "Good question" blurted out Jas and Chris at the same time. "We don't use money anymore; we use credit tokens or cards." Said Avery. "I can give you each a couple 100 token coins and you're going to have to make that work.

Once they access my bank and see transactions being made here they will know where I am. This is the weekend so even in our time; the transactions won't or shouldn't be discovered until Monday."
"Just look at others in the mall and get an idea of how they are dressing now and buy similar styles" added Avery. "See ya back here in 30" and with that he and Tommy were gone.

Jas and Sammy were the next couple to disappear into the crowd which only left Brett and me. He looked at me and said, "Well, shall we?" As if we were proceeding to the dance floor.

We looked around in the store we were hiding in first. As we eyed the other shoppers, I noticed Brett randomly grabbing articles of clothing from the shelves that looked similar to what others were wearing and hopefully they fit because I don't think he was checking sizes. I, on the other hand, wanted to be the best dressed alien in the time warp.

I looked and quickly deciphered what was hot fashion and made my choices carefully. Now, if this coin thing works we'll have some spare time to look around a little.

With our arms loaded down, Brett and I started for the register. It was weird. There was no cashier, just a self-checkout thing with a flat screen. I put the coin in what looked like a pay slot. A face came on the screen and said I had thirty credits remaining how would I like them? I didn't know what to say. Then the face on the screen asked again. "Would you like a coin back or a store credit?" I said "Coin back" and out rolled a coin from a coin release on the register. It was a thirty credit coin.

Just one coin for whatever denomination you're getting for change. No more pennies or purchases that end in cents. Just a flat fee of rounded off credits. "How cool is that?" I said to Brett as I turned to face him. What the heck? I thought he was right behind me. As I scanned the room I saw clothes racks, clothes hanging on the walls, flat screens playing music videos, a couple looking at belts hanging up in a corner. My eyes had almost made it all the way around the room before I saw Brett and of course there he was talking to a girl. It appeared she was giving him style tips. I grinned and started toward them.

About half way I felt like someone was coming up behind me but I shrugged it off. I was clearly focused on my destination and not the weirdness I felt as I got closer. Then almost simultaneously I saw the girl reaching for what looked like a gun or stun gun or something of that nature and the guy behind me put his hand on my shoulder and something cold touched my back. I reached out to signal Brett and I saw our eyes meet just before everything went black.

Sammy and Jasmine hadn't really talked much since graduation. The last three years they mostly kept up second hand. They were taking their time looking for clothes to change into and spent more time getting reacquainted. There was a huge aquarium filling the center of the mall from floor to ceiling. You could see it from every floor. Jas and Sammy walked around it from floor to floor taking the winding staircase that encircled it. They would stop periodically to check out clothes stores that caught their attention.

"Look", Jasmine yelled out. "I bet we could find something to wear in there." Sammy turned to see and it was a Buffalo Exchange store. Jas smiled at him "Remember when we used to get different clothes from here like every week?" "You mean *you* used to get clothes from here like every week. I traded some of my brother's clothes here a couple times and got me stuff for a laugh."

They entered the store. It was really different than they remembered. Now there was a flat screen as soon as you walked in with a rock-n- roll looking girl telling you how the Buffalo Exchange works. "Bring in your old clothes and trade them for any clothes of equal or lesser value or just get coins." The girl on the TV yelled out as we strolled past. Mostly they had retro or unusual fashions here.

Yep this was Jasmine's kind of place. "We can give up the clothes we're wearing and keep the coins for something else," said Jas. "They might take your clothes", said Sammy, but who's going to want my old jeans and t-shirt?" "Well let's look around any way", said Jas as she started flipping through the racks.

"Hey! Look at this," she said grinning from ear to ear as she pulled a dress out to show Sammy. But Sammy was not next to her. At first she was angry. Just like him she said to herself. Probably found a young salesgirl to flirt with. "This is exactly why we didn't work out!" She continued to talk to herself.

The more she looked around, she noticed she was the only one in the store. Now she was scared. A rush of butterflies filled her gut and not in a good way. She hung the dress back on the rack and slowly made her way to the entrance trying not to look nervous. She made it to the fish tank and grabbed tightly to the rail of the stairs. She found it hard to breath. Where was Sammy? He would not have left her alone like that. She felt overwhelmed with fear.

Just when she thought she would be stranded there someone grabbed her from behind and told her to run. It was Sammy! He pulled her into a spot under the stairs. "What are you doing?" She asked? "Where were you? What's going on? Tell me!!" She started to get louder.

Sammy put his hand over her mouth as she struggled to get it loose. "Stop!" Sammy yelled in a loud harsh whisper. "Someone tried to grab me in there and inject me with something. I fought it out of his hand and ran.

He came after me so I doubled back to get you. We have to hide somewhere. How do we get back to that store were we're supposed to meet up?"

"Do you really think it's a good idea to go back there? We don't know that it's safe there. I said from the beginning that we shouldn't have trusted that guy. This is like a crazy nightmare!" Jasmine said as she held back the tears. "We definitely need to get out of this area and try to find the others." She added. "Ok," Sammy said, "This is what we're going to do. Did you buy anything in that store?" "No," Jasmine replied, "There wasn't anyone to check me out so I got scared and left."

"Yea, well apparently they don't have cashiers anymore but that's ok. I found out the hard way." Sammy said with a halfcocked smile on his obviously terrified face. "We need to be able to blend in until we find everyone else. If this wasn't a random jacking, then all of us could be in danger. "Random jacking?!" Jas shouted in a quiet squeaky whisper. "What is that supposed to mean? Who injects someone to rob them?" "Look, all I know is that there are a lot of unfamiliar things here and we don't know what people are apt to do. We're not in Kansas anymore, babe.

I don't think it's a good idea to buy anything in this mall. There are cameras everywhere. If this was the cops, they're most likely watching for us to do that." Sammy told Jasmine as they both watched all directions with terror in her eyes.

Sammy holding Jasmine close to him bent down and kissed her forehead. She looked into his eyes as if this might be the last time they would ever be able to see each other again. He kissed her lips and they embraced each other as if letting go was not an option.

Eyes closed only for a second then once again wide open searching the area for any crouching enemies about to pounce.

Sammy grabbed Jasmine by the hand and led her out into the mall and told her they were going to breeze past the store they were supposed to meet up in to see if he could see anyone. If not, they were going to get the hell out of this mall and into the nearby neighborhood. Better to hide in plain sight he thought.

They headed toward the main entrance of the mall which would take them past the storefront. Both of them clinging tightly to one another, eyes peeled in every direction, continuously searching for any hint of danger for each step of the journey toward the storefront.

"There it is!" Jasmine blurted out. The main entrance was in sight. "I don't see anyone, do you?" said Sammy as they both could feel their hearts pounding out of their chests, palms sweaty and pace as fast as it could be without running. "I can't breathe" said Jasmine, "No, I don't see anyone. Keep going.

I just want to get out of here. I feel like a caged animal in here." "Another thirty feet" said Sammy. From here to the exit the only focus was on that door.

Just as we were about to set off the automatic doors, a hand grabbed Sammy's shoulder. Both Sammy and jasmine screamed out as they spun around; Sammy ready with fists clinched to break the two of them free from this predator that had possibly already kidnapped the rest of their party.

As he spun around ready for a fight; Tommy reared back to dodge the blow as he put his hands up saying, "Whoa! Dude! Calm down! What's going on? I thought you were supposed to be buying clothes and not going outside the mall. You seemed to be heading out of here pretty fast; I could hardly catch up to you.

At first I thought you were coming back to the store but when you blew past it I thought I better find out where you thought you were going." "At this point, *dude,* I don't know who you are or what is going on. All I know is someone tried to jack me up in this mall and we're getting the hell out of here!" Blasted Sammy.

"Where'd you come from anyway? I didn't see you when we passed the store. Where's your sidekick? I don't trust that guy for a minute but if he's near here you tell him Jas and I want to go back to our time right the fuck now and he can deal with finding his family without us!"

"Wait a minute," said Tommy, "What do you mean someone tried to what, jack you up?" "Where? How long ago? We need to tell Avery. Come on back to the store with me so we can find out what's going on." "No! I just told you I don't trust that guy. Why do you? I can't believe that you have taken his side on everything over your friends! I don't even know you right now. All I know is that if we don't get out of this mall something bad is going to happen. I have a really bad feeling about this."

"So do I," said Jasmine. "I am scared to death that I am never going to see my family again. When I was in the Buffalo Exchange I swear there was someone watching me. The hair was standing up on the back of my neck and I feel the same way right now. Can we just please continue this discussion outside?"

Tommy rolled his eyes and looked at the floor then he looked up and met eyes with Jasmine. With a deep sigh he asked "Have either of you seen Chris and Brett? One thing is for sure, we can't get back without that remote and them. Let's just go back where we know we're safe and talk to Avery."

"Avery, Avery, always Avery. I say we just gank that fucker and take that remote. We can't do anything in his safe zone. We need to get him out away from his support system." Argued Sammy.

"Are you hearing yourself?" Asked Tommy. "Who am I? Who are you? Since when are you a gangster? Wanting to rob someone?"

"Well," said Sammy, "Since someone tried to inject me with who knows what!" With that Sammy grabbed Jasmines' hand and they walked out of the mall leaving Tommy behind with his newly acquired best friend. As his friends disappeared out the door, Tommy was all alone in a time he didn't know if he would ever return from.

About that time Avery walked up behind him gnawing on his fingernails. He spit a sliver out of the side of his mouth and remarked that no one had come back to the store yet.

"We need to round everyone up and get moving," said Avery, "My friend came back and told me some disturbing news. I would like to talk to everyone at the same time. Why are we standing here staring at the exit?" He slapped the side of Tommy's arm and said, "Come on, we can't be out here. Let's go."

"They left," whispered Tommy as he turned to face Avery in a zombie like state, "They said someone tried to inject Sammy with something. Do you know anything about that? What are we doing here? It wasn't supposed to be like this. Have I involved my friends in something that could get them killed? We were just supposed to hide you out, not leap through time. None of us have seen Chris or Brett, for all I know, they're missing."

As Tommy brushed the stray hair out of his face he felt bewildered at himself for thinking more about the possibilities of this time machine than the well-being of his friends and himself. Now he was engulfed in immense hysteria that was stirring inside him like a tornado striking his internal organs with such force he was fighting the need to double over in pain.

How would he be able to fix this incomparable tragedy he had inflicted on his lifelong friends. Sammy was right; he was putting Avery and that remote in front of everything dear to him. He had to find his friends and Avery had to help him.

"We'll find our friends, said Avery, but not if we get caught as well. We need to get under cover so we can figure this thing out. I may be able to pull them back with us even though they aren't actually standing next to us, we are all still in the same dimension. Come on! Let's go!" Avery yelled out to Tommy who was still standing staring dumbfounded at the mall exit. Avery put his hand on Tommy's shoulder, "Dude let's go" he said in a soft less anxious tone. Tommy turned around and started back toward the store with Avery to hide in the back room and discuss a plan of action.

Once outside, Jasmine and Sammy walked the short distance to the nearby neighborhood. In their time; they had hung out there from time to time but now it was like somewhere they had never seen before and just as Avery had mentioned, the pollution was so bad you could hardly see down the streets.

Jas looked up at Sammy, "Are you sure we did the right thing? It's kind of scary out here. Where are we going to go?" "I don't know," said Sammy "But I was getting claustrophobic in there, weren't you?" "Yeah, and I can't believe Tommy! I've never seen him act like this before." Responded Jas. "I'm getting the feeling there is more to this thing than he's letting on." Said Sammy. "We need to find somewhere to sit down and get our bearings.

Hey look! They still have Seven Eleven's; let's sit there for a minute maybe get something to drink." Sammy sang out with a little more confidence as he grabbed Jasmine's hand and dragged her to the corner. "See," said Sammy, "Some things never change. I wonder how we use this money. You want to come in or sit out here?" "You must be crazy if you think I'm going to let you out of my sight," answered Jasmine. "Anyway, I'm curious to see if they still have Slurpies and Big Gulps." They both giggled as they entered the store.

Not much has changed in here they said almost in harmony as they made their way to the drink section.

"I told you everything was going to be ok," said Sammy. "We need to find out where that guy lives. What was his name? Freud? No, that's not it. What is it?"

"You mean Einstein?" Laughed Jas. "What's his name now? Oh yeah, Yancy." "That's it," yelled out Sammy, "We need to find that dude, Yancy." When he said that they both felt eyes watching them.

They were almost afraid to turn around. Slowly they looked at each other as if they were hatching a telepathic plan to make their getaway. Sammy turned around first and was ready to make a run for it only instead of trouble; it was a little old man with wild hair and a huge mustache.

"Dude!" Yelled out Sammy, "Are you him?" Jasmine turned around. "Excuse him" she said, "We are just looking for an old friend and he mistook you for him. We're sorry." She grabbed Sammy's arm and attempted to pull him away from the stranger.

"So, we are friends now are we?" Said the gentleman. "I don't recall ever meeting you two before. How is it you know who I am?" Jas and Sammy stood with their mouths almost touching the floor as they realized they were actually speaking to a man they believed to be dead.

He milled around gathering items from the shelves as they were frozen in their tracks with no idea what to say to him and no words forming even if they could speak.

Yancy seemed to be muttering to himself but they managed to make out the words, "If you want to talk to me you best follow me. Anyway, you don't want to be outside here after dark." He turned and faced us and said, "I am assuming you have met my associate, Avery and something has gone wrong, yes?" Sammy still couldn't speak but Jasmine managed to take a step in his direction and force out a word or two. "Yeah, uh yes. We got separated." "Well then we need to find a solution" said the little man as we guilelessly followed another stranger into who knows where, who knows what adventure.

Back at the mall, Tommy and Avery were trying to find a way to make the remote pick up everyone that traveled without them being present. The whereabouts of Chris and Brett were still unknown. "Maybe we should go into the neighborhood and look for Jas and Sammy", Tommy nervously blurted out. "At least we have some sort of idea which direction they went. I don't like us being separated like this. You never said we were going to split up." "Tommy!" Yelled out Avery, "Damn you're worse than, he took a deep breath, look, I'm sorry that this is not going as planned. You knew this thing was still experimental. I'm doing my best. If we could only find Yancy we might have a better chance. We can't stay here all night so I have to come up with something soon or..."

"Or what? I've never been homeless and I sure as hell don't want to be homeless in a place I don't know." "We're not going to be homeless; we just need to find Yancy that's all." About that time Avery's friend came running in all out of breath. "I saw them", he was panting so hard we could hardly understand what he was saying. "I saw your friends" he said as he pointed toward Tommy "and I saw Yance, they were together, walking toward the Westgate." The young man stood bent over with his hands on his knees, taking in great gasps of air trying to catch his breath as Tommy and Avery looked at each other wide eyed half smiling. Avery grabbed his equipment and jumped up from his chair. He looked at his friend putting a hand on his back, "You sure it was the Westgate?" The boy nodded his head up and down. Tommy just looked at both of them dumbfounded.

"What are you just sitting there for?" Yelled out Avery. "We need to get to the Westgate before they have a chance to bug out of there. The Westgate is a hotel walking distance from here next to the freeway. Come on dude, move it!" Avery continued as he hastily shoved all of his things in a backpack.

Tommy jumped up from his seat and the three of them fled out a back door which took them to the backside of the mall. "I know what the Westgate is," said Tommy "I just can't believe it's still there..." Once outside, Tommy realized what Avery was talking about back at the house when he said it was overtaken by pollution on that side of town. The day was so hot and sunny and most everything looked the same. Fewer trees than his time but the same buildings still stood. He guessed they would be historical landmarks now. The only real difference was the smog. You couldn't see the freeway but knew which direction to go.

Hiding inside anywhere seemed crazy to him since there was literally no way anyone could see you outside in this cloud of poison.

They walked a normal pace as not to be noticeable to those searching for anyone out of place. The young man that accompanied them walked a couple paces behind them which Tommy thought was somewhat strange. He was a good looking kid with a nice personality. No doubt a new breed of goon geek groupie of the great Einstein.

He was tall and thin with a shaggy head of hair covered by Rastafarian looking hat. He wore a tank and jeans that looked like they had not been changed in a few days if not weeks. Flip flops on his feet exposing a pierced big toe which was a new one for me. All in all though, he really didn't look bad.

Tommy must have been looking a little too long at the kid because Avery slapped him in the arm to get his attention and just smiled as if to say stop staring.

"I was just wondering why he is staying so far back from us. I kinda feel like I'm being stalked," said Tommy.

"These days you have to travel like wolves. In a pack but where at least one lays back so if you get confronted they won't see him coming," replied Avery. "I guess it's just something we do almost reflexively now."

"We're almost to the hotel", said Avery. "How can you tell?" Tommy replied, "I can't see two feet in front of me."

"I can hear the freeway. Don't you hear it? I guess we've gotten accustomed to traveling by sonar," Avery said with a little snicker as he looked back at his friend. It seemed like his friend was wired for sound though since he gave little response to the comment.
We only walked about ten feet further when I could make out the Westgate hotel in front of us.
We made our way into the lobby and looked around.

"The Westgate was one of the nicest hotels in the area back in my time." Tommy said as his head tilted back looking at the ceiling and to each side observing the less than impressive interior.

The carpet was dirty and the wallpaper had started to peel in some areas. I guess the smog had stained everything in the area with this film of brown, like a house with multiple smokers.

Avery and his sidekick scoped out the area looking for Yancy. I was only concerned with looking for Jas and Sammy. If I could only find them, the four of us could start looking for Brett and Chris.
I gazed across the room once more as Avery was talking to someone at the front desk. I wondered if by the standards of the time this was still considered a nice place.

There were flowers in vases on nice tables but even the flowers looked brown to me. I saw people sitting in areas waiting to check in and drink stations for their convenience and.

Wait! There they are! I reached behind me to grab Avery but he wasn't in reach. I didn't want to take my eyes off them. I didn't want to call to them and draw attention either. I stood frozen with uncertainty a couple of seconds before I finally decided to quickly walk toward them, but they were on the other side of a very large room with people milling about. I was sure I would lose sight of them before I made it across the room. I felt like I was on the high school football field again trying to dodge the other team as I made my way to the end zone.

It was as if I was moving in slow motion. I clearly saw the suitcase I tripped over but a reaction to step over it didn't reach my brain fast enough. I suspect my collision must have gotten their attention because as I picked myself up from the floor, they were standing over me laughing and pointing.

No apologies needed to be expressed. We all knew that this was not the time to dwell on what we had said to one another at the mall. Now was the time to pull together and find our friends and get back to our time.

"Tommy", said Jasmine, "I am so glad to see you! I'd like you to meet…" "Yes, I know who that is"; Tommy said as he picked himself up from the floor and extended his hand. Nice to meet you Mr. Einstein, he said. Yancy pulled his hand away quickly and raised it up palm out waiving it back and forth. "Please", he said, "Yancy is my name, my friend." He delivered a little wink from his eye. "Now, do you know where my partner Avery is?"

I could see Avery and his friend approaching from behind Yancy. As my eyes rose above his head, Yancy turned to see his partner and friend coming in for a hug.

"I have a room and we need to get out of sight." Yancy whispered into Avery's ear as he motioned for the rest of us to follow. All the rooms were inside rooms but there were only three floors. Yancy's room was on the first floor towards the back of the hotel. As we approached the door I was expecting one of those credit card keys but now they use thumb print identification. Pretty cool I thought to myself.

Yancy slowly opened the door to his room which exposed what I would call a larger than average room for a hotel without being a suite. No one said a word as we piled in.

Avery was the last one in and shut the door and locked it with the deadbolt. He took a long deep breath and let it out.

As he walked down the short entryway into the main room he and Yancy stared at each other. "Mein alter freund. I never thought I'd see you again." Cried out Yancy. "I know it's only been a couple of months but when you get to be my age, a couple months could make a big difference." He chuckled a little. But it's been more than a couple months for you ja? Questioned the old man looking into Avery's eyes as if he was trying to see his soul.

"How is Temper? And the baby? Her family is really making a lot of trouble for both of us." I still don't understand why you didn't tell them the truth about where you were going."

Avery started to cry, "Yancy, Temper and Shaila are lost in time somewhere and I know you said not to try to travel back but Shaila is sick and I didn't know what else to do.

I thought we could come and find you and you might have some idea what's happening to her and what to do to make her well." He looked around the room at all of us and wiped the tears from his eyes. "I'm afraid I've drug these young people into my quandary as well.

They have two friends that may have been taken by the police. All we know is they were in the mall with us and now they're gone."

Yancy sat in a large Victorian chair that was part of the rooms' décor twisting on his mustache. He would twist the ends and stick them in his mouth, and then he would pull it out and point it toward us as if he were going to say something. He was apparently arguing in his mind about how to begin to fix this much escalated and potentially dangerous mess we have all gotten ourselves and him into.

All we could do is sit quietly and stare as one of the greatest minds in the world went to work. It was actually quite exciting. As Yancy and Avery discussed the possibilities of redesigning the time machine device to be able to locate someone; sort of like looking them up on a computer in a search engine on the technology of our time, they laid plans to make the device able to not only locate, but somehow catch them and move them from time to time as well as location to location. Mostly none of us understood the words they were using but knew it sounded brilliant.

Jasmine sitting on the bed next to me leaned over and whispered, "Tommy, maybe when we get back, I'll change my major to rocket science." She snickered a little but I think she was serious because I was thinking the same thing. Then Sammy who was sitting in a chair next to the bed leaned into the conversation and added his usual cynical remark "You mean *IF* we get back." With that we just sat quietly and watched the masters at work.

Eventually Jasmine lay back on the bed and fell asleep. We were all getting bored, tired and restless. As the clock ticked away, all I could think about was what could be going on with Brett and Chris.

Who could or would have taken them? If no one took them, why would they leave the mall? So many things were running through my head, I couldn't for the life of me understand how Jas could sleep but then I realized even though it was early afternoon here we had actually been up for quite some time.

I looked at Yancy and Avery diligently working on their scientific shit, the kid sleeping in a chair, and Sammy in on the crapper, I pushed Jas over and laid back on the bed next to her. Only she was fast asleep and I was staring at the ceiling drifting back to happier times when we were younger and things were more predictable.

I remember right before graduation when once again Jasmine caught Sammy with some girl from a school in the next district. She was so done with him and never going to talk to him again. Brett and I took her out to Thrasher Land to watch Chris compete in some skateboard thing and he was awesome.

He looked like poetry in motion as he rolled up one side grabbing his board when he reached the top flying high into a summersault then hitting back down without a care in the world only to roll back up the other side and do it again. I swear I could watch him all day and never get bored. This particular time though, Jasmine was nonstop ranting about Sammy.

Brett and I were really sick of hearing it. Sammy may have been bad at monogamy but he was still our friend. Well, we were just about to cut her loose when Brett interrupted and dared her to try skateboarding. Of course, she cannot let a dare go unanswered and actually rented one.

I remember her saying something about "It's not so hard" and "She's good with balance", right before she went down the tube and broke her arm.

Chris was finished competing by this time and the three of us took her to the hospital. It was a clean break but it kept her from cheering for the rest of basketball season. I remember how angry Sammy got with us for letting her get on a skateboard. It was always little endearing things like that keeping us so close for so many years.

It was like whenever we were thinking about trying to grow up and head our own direction, something always happened and pulled us back together. I must have dozed off thinking about that because the next thing I know Jasmine was shaking me telling me to stop talking in my sleep. I opened my eyes to see everyone stopped in their tracks looking at me.

"Well, sleeping beauty, are you awake now? Can we go get your friends or would you like to relax in this hotel room a little longer?" Said the unequivocal German accented Yancy.

"We think we've had a bit of a breakthrough here," jumped in Avery. "We think we have configured the TM (time machine) to be able to relocate us by, hmmm well he grinned, there are a lot of big words I could use but basically the thing will pick up a lock on their DNA and carry us to within hopefully fifty feet of them. There is only one problem. The cosmos in all their wonder have a very strict molecular structure and what that means to us is that if something moves into a space, something else has to move out of that space. It is possible if we hit too close, it could bump them somewhere else unknown."

"With that being said, we, Yancy and I think it would be best if only two of us went in." Yancy put his hand on Avery's shoulder seemingly reassuring him that it would be okay to breathe as the biggest obstacle had been overcome and who to take was a decision that would happen generically. Avery looked down understanding the gesture. He looked at Yancy then scanned the room full of his new friends. The kid must have taken off while Jas and Tommy slept which left only three choices of who would travel with Avery since Yancy made it clear it would not be him.

"Um," Sammy looked at Tommy, "I think this is where we need to draw straws or something, is that what you're insinuating, Avery? You want us to decide who's going with you or did you already know who you want? And while I have the floor, I'm not clear on this whole DNA tracking system you braniacs hit on. I thought you needed a semen sample or some sort of body fluid to find DNA."

"That's right, it used to be only body fluid that could run DNA in your time," responded Yancy, but we have recently, and this is common knowledge today, recently found that body fluid is what keeps the body running like gasoline in a car, right, well when you put gas in your car and run it the engine heats up, follow me?

Once it heats up the steam or fumes penetrate the vehicle and can be detected. Well this is similar to a car's engine in the process that as the body burns its fluids it secretes a heat induced fume, if you will, that is in fact a gaseous form of DNA that I have been able to make traceable with this device. Anyone not understanding me?" Yancy and Avery looked around at a roomful of head scratches and dumbfounded expressions.

Jasmine was the first to utter her input. She shook her head dismissing the whole theory of DNA as something that she would never understand so there was no point in dwelling on the subject.

"I really want to find Chris and Brett but I'm not sure if this particular leap is for me. You guys might run into trouble and need a man to deal with it. I'm just saying... we don't know who took them, or do we?"

"We actually don't know if anyone took them for sure," replied Avery. "It just seems like logical thinking since someone tried to assault Sammy around the same time." "I've talked to my friend at the store and they haven't shown back up there either, so that's a pretty good indication that they didn't just go exploring."

Avery raised his eyebrows and shrugged his shoulders as he looked around the room. Jasmine looked at the floor since she had already taken herself out of the running for who would go with Avery to find Chris and Brett. Tommy who was propped against the nightstand with his arms folded across his chest looked at Sammy who was returning a look of wide eyed determination.

Not looking away from Tommy, Sammy asked, "Would it be ok for Jasmine to stay with Einstein, I mean Yancy and both of us go with you?" With that statement, Sammy turned and looked at Jasmine. "I don't want you to be left alone here and I think we both may need to go in case, like you said, there could be trouble."

Everyone looked at Yancy who was sitting in a chair, legs crossed, playing with his mustache. His eyes widened as if to say, why is everyone looking at me?

He cleared his throat and gained his composure and looked at Jasmine. "Do you think you could shtand the company of an old man for der auben, mien shotze?" He said with a smile as he tilted his head. His warm unshakable approach made her close her gaping mouth and smile back. "It would be my honor," she said and everyone for one split second smiled with warmth in their hearts and forgot that this leap without Jasmine could mean that they may never see her again.

"Well, that's it then," said Avery as he fumbled the time machine around in his hand. "Let's go find our friends." With that he pushed the button to send them on their way. One minute they were in the room together, the next there was only Jasmine and Yancy. "Wow," said Jasmine, "That was a new experience."

"Vas ist das?" Said Yancy as he gathered his paperwork. "I never thought about what was happening to the time you left behind. I never thought about how the abrupt removal of people in a confined space could make such a difference in the whole atmosphere of a room. I don't know exactly how to describe it but it's like I can still smell them only as quickly as I blinked my eyes they were gone and it kind of sucked the air out of the room. I guess I'm babbling and probably not making any sense."

"No," answered Yancy, "In fact you have explained it quite effectively. The air was in fact sucked out of der room when they left because das space they inhabited with the air was removed, thus causing a hole that needed to be filled by what air was left causing you and me to feel the movement of atmospheric reconstruction. Now we just sit and wait for them to reappear. In the meantime, I'm going to try to find a way to locate Temper and Shaila. Did you know them?"

"No," said Jasmine, "I only met Avery a day or two ago. At least I think it's only been a day or two. With all that has gone on in the time since I met him, it seems like much longer." I wonder what's happening with them."

"Best not to think about it, you'll drive yourself crazy. Come help me with this gizmo, fraulein." Yancy said with his soft animated tone.

What a relaxing way he had about him, thought Jasmine. Like nothing is so bad it can't be fixed with nothing more than time to find the right formula. And he had all the time in the world.

The guys had made their leap and found they had made a lateral move only a couple miles from the hotel. "That wasn't a leap, fuck, we could have taken a taxi." said Sammy, "That was more of a teleportation." "We could have fucking walked here!"

"You mean we risked bumping Chris and Brett into oblivion to go somewhere we could have walked or taken Citi transit to?" Tommy angrily blurted out. "Dude! I am really growing tired of this game!" With that Avery grabbed him by the front of his shirt and pulled him close to his face.

"You think this is a game! Do you! My wife and daughter are out there somewhere and I should be looking for them instead we're here looking for your friends who would not be in this spot if they had just done what they were told! This is not a game!" he repeated, voice reaching abnormal octaves as the frustration, anger and fear for his family all came rushing out.

He gave another yank to Tommy's shirt and said as he stared into his eyes trying to get a grip on his emotions, "We need to keep our voices down and scope this place out." He let go of the shirt and they looked around to see if there were any signs of anything they could call a clue to where they should go to find Chris and Brett.

They started to surround the house they were led to by the DNA locator when they heard faint talking. It sounded like Chris. Who was he talking to and where was Brett? Avery motioned for Sammy to take the back of the house while he took the front and Tommy lay back out of sight.

Tommy could see Avery but Sammy disappeared around the back. There was a loud crashing sound then Avery went running toward the rear of the house. Tommy didn't know if he should follow or wait for a sign. He frantically paced back and forth straining his ears for a signal to step in or something. He was about to reveal himself when he saw Chris and Brett come running out the front door.

Tommy whistled to get their attention but it looked as though they were running blind, but from who or what? Tommy took off through the neighborhood after them calling out to them.

As he ran past the house and saw the door was open and he saw a couple men moving about but not Sammy or Avery. He chased after Chris and Brett for at least a mile before they stopped to catch their breath. As he approached he could hear them promising each other to get back in shape. When Tommy ran up on them they started to take off again until they saw who it was.

"Damn it!" Brett forced out amidst his huffing and puffing. "Where the hell did you come from? I thought it was one of those bastards following us. Shit! Why didn't you identify yourself?" He said as the sweat poured down his face like a fountain and he bounced around like a runner that just finished a heat.

"I don't care where he came from", wheezed out Chris. "I'm just happy as shit to see someone I know other than Brett. No offense, dude." "None taken," he replied as he put his hand on Chris' back who was still bent over holding his knees trying to breathe.

"We'd better get moving before they catch up with us." "Before who catches up with you? Who was in that house? How did you get there? Why did you leave the mall? Fuck! You two! We've been worried as shit! We need to go back to the house to get Sammy and Avery. We came here to rescue you two."

"How did you know where to find us? We don't even know where we are," asked a confused Chris.

"We were in that store shopping for something to wear and the next thing we knew we were in that house with some stupid looking inbreeds asking us all kinds of questions about our fucking time capsule."
"The time capsule?" Tommy repeated with a suspicious tone.

"Wait a minute; Avery said he found us through the time capsule. Oh my God," his knees went weak, the hair on the back of his neck stood up. Did those inbreeds have a name? Did they say anything that made any sense at all?" "Dude, they drugged us or something. It's all a blur." Replied Chris.

"There's something else going on here. That time capsule must mean something else in this time. We need to go back to that house and find Sammy and if possible, question those inbreeds."

"Find Sammy? Asked Chris, "What's he doing at that house?" "He was with me trying to rescue you two fucktards. Avery and Yancy invented something to locate your fricken body fluids." They all had a little giggle that quickly turned to serious determination to find out why they were really there and do their best to get home. All of them.

The afternoon was still blistering hot but the sun was barely visible because of the pollution. They started walking back toward the house where Brett and Chris had been held but about half way there they ran into Avery and Sammy who were looking a little out of breath.

"What happened?" asked Chris who was over the top with anxiety. "Who were those guys? Why did they take us and why were they interested in our time capsule?" Brett and

Sammy looked at Chris in amazement, and then looked at each other. He was usually the one that went with the flow and rarely got excited about anything. He was way over the top. I don't think anyone had ever seen him like that before.

"Damn Chris," said Sammy, "Calm down, dude. You're going to hyperventilate. Take a breath! Shit! You're ok".

Chris ran his fingers through his hair and took a deep breath and let it out long and hard. Then he kind of halfway forced out a smile as he extended his right hand out to show everyone how it was shaking from the experience he had just endured. He turned his back to us as he linked his fingers together behind his head and tried to regain his composure.

Seeing that he was pulling himself together, we turned our attention to Avery who seemed to be working an equation in his head and talking to himself in a muffle.

He must have felt the weight of our stares because he looked up and started biting his fingernail. His words said he was as curious and stunned as us about the whole abduction but his eyes said something else, at least to Sammy.

Tommy was and always had been too trusting. He was like an engineer in that he was interested in the time machine and how it works and assumed Avery was telling him the truth and we were not in danger.

"We need to get back to the hotel and check on Jasmine", said Sammy. He was going to play it cool but going to be more cautious from now on. Something was not right about this whole scenario.

"I think from now on," continued Sammy, "We should not split up for any reason." "I second that," chimed in Brett. "That was definitely some hardcore shit right there. And if you can find people now by their body juice or whatever, you should be able to find your family and we can go home. Yea, let's get Jas and end this nightmare."

Everyone but Avery was nodding their heads up and down as to agree with Brett. They headed back towards the hotel. Sammy had one eye on his friends the other on Avery.

When they get back to the hotel, there was going to be a lot of explaining to do. Sammy hung back a few steps to keep an eye on the group altogether while his mind envisioned several different scenarios of what could be going on that they were not being made aware of and how did the time capsule fit in. He wondered if they would ever see their homes again. That two miles seemed to go on forever, no one was uttering a word.

None of them had been able to change clothes so they stuck out like Martians but no one gave that a thought. They were like zombies, exhausted, confused, and hungry unable to even focus on how to get themselves out of the mess they were in. They felt like prisoners of war in a foreign land.

Phoenix had really changed and not for the better. It was quite scary not being able to see too far ahead and there were peering eyes around every corner.

It was like a scary movie scene with creatures of the night following you in the shadows except it was daytime and they were people. Mostly homeless alley dwellers and addicts looking for a quick fix and a way to pay for it.

"Shit!" burst out Brett to everyone's surprise, "Where the hell is Cortez?" "Cortez?, interrupted Chris, "We're only at Cortez? I think this is way further than two miles." He added. "That's all you have to say? Cortez was a landmark a historical building!" Interjected Brett. "Alice Cooper went to school there for Christ's sake, how could they tear that down?"

"Who is she," Asked Avery? "I was a history minor and I never heard of her." Everyone chuckled out loud except for Avery who was oblivious to how crazy he sounded to them not knowing who Alice Cooper was, especially coming from Phoenix.

"Dude," interrupted Chris, "She is a he and in our time and a bit before that Alice Cooper was an awesome singer and actually a pioneer to a fashion that lingered for quite a few years.

He was iconic in his musical style and showmanship which opened up a whole new platform for rock and roll; plus he grew up in Phoenix and had an awesome house up on Pinnacle Peak that overlooked like most of the West side and part of the East. In our time, this high school was famous, now it's gone?"

"Well, it's not like any of us went there," said Tommy. "I don't think I know anyone that went there for that matter." "Sure you do," popped out Chris with a big smile on his face.

Tommy and Brett both looked at him like they were searching the far recesses of their memory to figure out who it was.

"Come on you guys, think," Chris said as his smile turned to an outright laugh. "Think, tall, red hair, beautiful tan..." Then Tommy obviously remembered and burst into laughter.

"Ah ha ha, now I remember, wow, ha ha ha yea, that was a night from hell!"
Brett was still looking dumbfounded but smiling.

"I don't know who you're talking about." He said still trying to recall. Chris and Tommy turned and looked at Sammy who was a few feet behind them.

"You remember Cortez High School don't you, Sammy?" yelled Chris. He just waved his hand in a manner that said 'leave it alone'. Tommy and Chris turned back to Brett and told him and Avery about a girl Sammy picked up at a party that Brett was grounded and couldn't go to. She was so pretty with long straight red hair and dark tan.

She was tall and green eyes that were just captivating. "Sammy bet us that she would be with him by the end of the night so all night we watched him work his charm and all night she wasn't having it," said Chris.

"Yea," Tommy interrupted, "And then she finally said she would go with him and she would meet him in the parking lot. By this time she was wasted," continued Tommy with more laughter and animation.
So we all decided to go to Jack-in-the-Box and get something to eat, right." By this time everyone had stopped walking and was looking at Sammy.
Sammy started waving his arms as if to tell them to stop telling the story, but Chris continued.

"Do you want to tell the rest?" Asked Chris who was laughing so hard he had everyone laughing even Sammy. "Ok," Sammy gave in, "She wolfed down a nasty looking burger in seconds flat dropping half of it in her lap then she sucked down a shake without taking a breath. You don't even want to know what happened next." "Come on," said Avery, "I love stories like this."

"Well, she was wearing this short top with this matching low rider short skirt and cowboy boots. I mean she was hot" Sammy said as he nodded towards Tommy and Chris for confirmation. "No doubt," said Chris "Totally hot." "Anyway," Sammy went on, "She started looking all pale and we knew she was going to hurl so we tried to direct her to the ladies room but on the way," he stopped dead in his tracks. "What?" Yelled Brett, "did she puke, you guys never told me this story before" "No," Sammy said with a much more solemn face that turned to a really grossed out face. "She bent over like she was going to throw up but sharted on Sammy's leg!" blurted out Chris who was laughing so hard we could barely understand what he was saying. "Oh, no! That is nasty!" Said Brett. "What did you do?"

"I went into the men's room and cleaned it off my leg and left the bitch there. That was the last time I ever picked up anyone from that fucking school", said Sammy no longer laughing. Everyone else was laughing hysterically.

In an effort to change the subject, Sammy reminded them they were on their way to the hotel and should get moving. Everyone agreed and resumed their journey. As they passed the mall, Avery's lanky friend joined them on their walk. He stayed back with Sammy but didn't say a word. As they approached the room, Jasmine must have heard them coming down the hall because she bounced out the door to greet them.

"Chris, Brett, I'm so glad to see you're OK!" She shouted as she grabbed both of them in a group hug. "I was so worried" she added as she slapped Brett across the chest. "What happened to you? Where have you been?"
Avery herded everyone into the room. "You don't want to linger in these halls too long". He said as we all headed inside.
Yancy was sitting in the same spot as when everyone left. He had some instruments and strange formulas written on a sheet of paper.

He looked up and out the top of some magnifying glasses siting on the end of his nose and said, "Kommen sie bitte, sitzen. I might have found somezing."

"Have you located Temper and Shaila?" Avery said almost trembling. He started chewing his fingernails as Yancy explained.

"According to der information you gave me und der formula I have been working on, if the problem was solved correctly, he snickered a little, I can at least tell you vat year they are in and possibly put you in der same time zone. The rest dear fruend, vill be up to you." He smiled as if he had just invented the wheel.

Jasmine nudged Sammy as her heart filled with excitement not only for the joy that Avery was feeling at the thought of recovering his family but also for the fact that history was being made in that hotel room and even though it was the future, they were part of it.

She wished she had known Einstein or even paid more attention in school when they were studying him. He was the real deal and yet acted like a regular guy. The whole time she was alone with him, he kept her up to speed on what he was doing and put it in terms she could understand. Not once did he make her feel mentally inferior.

Brett snapped his fingers in front of Jasmines face to bring her back to reality. "You back," Brett said as she slapped his fingers away. "Looked like you left us for a minute there. You ok?" He smiled and teased.

Sammy walked toward the chair Jas was sitting in and leaned against the nightstand close enough to be able to rest against her. He was always conscious of her and always let her know he was there for her. This was understood and no words needed to be spoken, it was obvious Avery was anxious as were we all to go back home and let him go his own way and find his family.

Yancy was explaining to him what the formula was and how to use it when all of a sudden there was a loud noise in the hallway. It sounded like an army was running through. I think we all noticed at the same time that it seemed to stop abruptly in front of our room. You could just see everyone in the room deflate with the realization that we were with a man wanted for murder and no way out except that door.

"Oh, shit", whispered Sammy. "What the fuck?" That was the last thing any of us heard.

Chapter 3

The Search for Temper and Shaila

As we all became aware we had just been bumped through time again, you could hear Jasmine scream out like someone had just come up from behind and frightened her, Tommy was holding back vomit, no wait, vomiting, Sammy was yelling out profanities and the rest of us were just trying to get our bearings.

"You have got to stop doing that without any warning," yelled out Sammy to Avery. "And what was that back there? Were there police at our door?"

"I believe zey ver federal agents looking for Avery." came a familiar voice from behind a dumpster. We all went running around to see Yance sitting on the curb with his hands on his knees, shaking his head back and forth slowly. I never vanted to come back to das time but I guess I was shtanding too close to der signal." He said raising his hand to scratch his head.

"Vell, now since I am here vie vill just have to make sie best of it. I did not vant to go through another interrogation anyway." "So, das this look familiar to anyone?"

We all stood looking around for a minute trying to decide if we knew where we were. "These neighborhoods all look alike," said Chris as he started walking toward the corner of the intersection to see if there was a street sign or something, anything, familiar. "Dudes, he yelled out. I think we're at Sun City, I see a bunch of golf carts at the front of this plaza."

"Why the fuck would you zap us to Geizerville?" Asked Brett. "How we going to get back to our side of town? They don't run Citi transit this far out."

"Vas ist das Geizerville??" Asked Yancy. Everyone looked at Avery for answers since he was the one holding the remote.

Yancy looked up at Avery and gave a reassuring nod and wink. Avery's eyes got wide and you could see the vulnerability in them like we had never seen before.

"The remote was programmed to take us to Temper," he said almost as if he were trying to convince himself that it could be the end of his search. "She must be around here somewhere close," he said. "Everyone OK enough to walk?"

"We should grab a newspaper and verify what day and year it is before we just go walking around, shouldn't we," asked Jasmine. "Is that crazy or was anyone else curious?"

"No, that's an excellent idea" Tommy said. "Anyone have money?" He looked around and saw Jasmine going through her purse and the guys all reaching into their pockets. No one seemed to be pulling anything out though. "OK," said Tommy, "We can look at the paper in the store without buying it. At least get a date off of it."

Chris stopped dead with his hand in his pocket and a sort of weird look on his face. "Those federal agents," he hesitated and looked at Yancy, "Um they can't come here, can they? I mean, they won't, right?" Everyone stopped what they were doing and awaited an answer as they turned their attention toward Yancy and Avery.

Yancy shrugged his shoulders and raised one eyebrow. "Who knows vat they are capable of," Yancy replied. "They took most of my notes from my lab and vere asking a lot of questions about vat vas I working on. I cannot guarantee they do not have the same device to travel through time with, however, they for sure cannot follow us mitout knowing vat year and location to select."

"If they do find a way to track us", added Avery, "One thing is for sure, they would stop at nothing to eliminate me and possibly anyone who helps me."

Jasmine started to shake uncontrollably and hyperventilate. Sammy put his arm around her and told her it would be ok. "How is that ok? He just told us they were going to kill us if they found us. This is Tommy's fault," she cried.

"Tommy brought him into our lives! How could you put us in danger like this?" She screamed at Tommy. Sammy just hugged her close and reassured her it was not going to turn out like that. He promised. She pushed him away and walked to the curb and sat down putting her head in her hands muttering that no one could keep a promise like that.

Sammy turned to Tommy raising his hand gesturing that she would be alright just give her a minute to regroup. Sammy may have been playing mediator and pretending what he said was sincere but he was as afraid as everyone else that this may not end well.

"Those police are after you for killing your wife and kid, right?" Interjected Brett. "So all we have to do is find them and they will have no other charges, right? I say we start looking. That remote brought us here because it detected her DNA. Now, does that mean she is here or has been here? I mean, I'm no scientist but how long does that residue hang around? Is it like perfume or does it have to be on a warm body to be detected? I'm just thinking out loud here."

"Zat is very scientific und profound thinking young man," chimed in Yancy, "und a very good question. My first response vould be dat it vould have to be on the body to be detectable but it might be possible dat residue could linger for no more than a few seconds I vould tink. But we know it may take only a few seconds to get very far away especially if all of us bumping in dis spot at der same time bumped her out.

For sure she was here nearby or was she exactly here and had to vacate der space to make room for us? Dat ist a very good question indeed," the old man said as he walked around to the front of the plaza scratching his head.

We all pondered on his words for a second and tried to picture the scenario. Avery started to get a worried but determined look on his face. Jasmine, as usual was sitting looking at us with her mouth hanging open. Then Brett asked, "Has anyone seen Chris?" No one had noticed that he was missing until then. He was one of those guys that were not really there even when he was there; you know the one that is always preoccupied with shit going on in his own world that he's never really cognizant of his present surroundings. "Maybe he went to see what year it is," said Jas as she dragged herself up from the curb.

We all started heading around to the front of the plaza when we saw Chris and Yancy standing in front of one of the stores talking to a crowd of senior citizens.

We approached the crowd and found that we had stumbled into the year 2018 and it was Cinco de Mayo and they were gathering at the plaza for a parade that was going to be happening later in the morning. The plaza was more like a little strip mall where Party City was the main store. Party City was where the parade would begin and end after circling the small community. These people were part of the parade and were driving their golf carts. They had made trays of food which would be available after the parade ended. Then they usually had a block party well into the evening with fireworks.

"This could be good," said Avery. "If Temper and Shaila are here they may come out for the party or even the food if they are out of cash and hungry."

"Did you say Temper and Shaila?" Came a little voice from the crowd. "Yes", Avery quickly replied. "Do you know someone by that name?"

A little old woman emerged through a hole in the crowd carrying a Chihuahua. My husband and I were supposed to meet them here around ten o'clock. Lovely girl that Temper is and her daughter is priceless. We met them walking down the old town road about a week ago and they looked lost so we stopped and gave them a ride into town.

We ran into them a couple days later at the gas station washing up and it was obvious to us they had no place to stay and they looked hungry too, so we asked them to come have lunch with us. Well, after we spent the afternoon with them we just couldn't let them sleep outside so we asked them if they'd like to stay in the spare room.

Then a little old man walked up behind her and put his arm around her. "Yep," he said, "Our grandson was staying with us but he moved out about two years ago and we had his room empty ever since." The old woman interrupted him with a look like it was her story, let her tell it. Even the dog gave him a look. She said her husband was coming to get her but he had been delayed and they ran out of money.

"I reckon you're the husband", blurted out the old man. Again with a glance from the wife. He just scratched on his head and looked away. "Anyway," the old woman continued, "She is meeting us here any time now."

Everyone looked at Avery who was beaming with his chest out and a wild smile unable to be tamed.

"Vell," said Yancy, "vile you are waiting for Temper, I vill look around at der booths and pick out vat I vill be eating ven der parade is over. Anyone care to join me."

As we all expected, Avery was not leaving the side of that old couple and of course Tommy right by his side. The rest of us followed Yancy. As we walked along looking at booths of pies, treats, and crafts, we heard a woman screaming as she ran through the crowd pulling a child behind her. "OMG!" Jasmine yelled out. "Is that her?"

We all turned to see a very pretty woman pushing her way through the crowd shouting out "Avery!"

We all turned to see the look on Avery's face as she ran to embrace him but all we saw were the old man and woman.

We turned back to Temper as she yelled out "No! God no, please, no, no." She fell to her knees crying and clinching tightly to her daughter as a few bystanders gathered around her. "Are you all right, miss?" one woman asked.

Temper stood up and by this time the old couple was upon her sheltering her from the onlookers. As she reassured the couple that she had just tripped over her own foot she was scanning the crowd hoping that he was still here. Instead she spotted Yancy. Their eyes met as we all stood watching her wondering as well what happened to Avery and Tommy.

"What just happened?" Said Chris as all of us turned our heads in poetic motion without a reply. No one uttered a sound for at least a minute. It was obvious to us we had just witnessed what happens after we leap. The old couple seemed to have no recollection of Avery and Tommy even being there. We were stunned and bewildered.

We turned back to Temper as she said a few words to the couple and slowly worked her way through the crowd until she reached Yancy. They stood looking at each other for a second then Yancy put out his hand and called her by name. That was all it took for her to completely break down. She grabbed so tightly around Yancy's neck he could barely breathe as she held him there trying to get words out through her hysterical crying. Her daughter had a white knuckle grip on her mother's shirt.

"What, why, how did, damn it Yancy, what just happened?" She finally got out. Yancy pried her from around his neck and held her chin. "Mein shotze, are you ok?" "Yes," she said as she wiped the tears and took a deep breath. She unclenched her daughter from her shirt and held her hand. She took another deep breath and asked again. "I saw him, Yancy. I saw him then he was gone. What happened? Where did he go and why?"

"I can only guess at vat could have happened. I believe someone else bumped them out ven they arrived. I don't know who or how zey got der technology to do zis."

As he spoke Temper all of a sudden realized Yancy was not alone and she started looking at all of us and probably wondering why we were listening to their conversation and once more why was Yancy allowing us to hear about a secret she thought only they shared.

Jasmine saw her curiosity was peaked and extended her hand to the confused woman. "Hi, my name is Jasmine and these are my friends, Chris, Brett, and Sammy. We are friends of Avery from 2016. He found us through…" "The time capsule," Temper interrupted. She shook Jasmine's hand and seemed to accept that if Yancy was allowing them to know, it must be ok. About that time, Shaila began to turn a clammy looking color and doubled over in pain.

"Vie came here to find you because Avery said Shaila was not well. Vie need to figure dis out before anymore leaping. Hopefully vie can reverse der damage before it gets any worse. Is der anywhere vie can go away from dis crowd? Asked Yancy.

"There is a bridge about two miles from here. The underpass is covered by bushes. We stayed there a week and I never saw a car. We should be safe there or do you need a bed? We didn't have money and they still use it in this time. Does anyone have money?" We all shook our heads. "Well, the bridge it is," She said.

We headed in the direction of the bridge unaware that Avery and Tommy were bumped out by the same men that abducted Chris and Brett. The men were missing a valuable piece of the time travel puzzle and were convinced it was somehow connected to the time capsule. Two miles in this Arizona heat seemed more like ten. By the time we reached the bridge we were all happy to see some sort of shade but were totally unprepared to see what Temper had done to make it livable.

We pulled back the bushes to enter the underpass and it was like stepping into a living room inside a home. As everyone came through all you could hear was wow, holy shit, and daaaamn.

Usually under a bridge is dark and dirty but this one was lighted with battery operated lanterns, there were wall to wall rugs and nice ones, not dirty ones someone had thrown out. There was a coffee table, some chairs and a blow up mattress with sheets and a blanket. There was even a battery operated fan. Did I also say this was no low lying bridge; it had a ceiling of probably seven feet.

"How did you get der geld to furnish dis vundebar hideout?" asked Yancy. We were all so amazed that we couldn't speak. There were no bugs that we could see.

The only thing missing was running water and a toilet but then there was plenty of outside for that and plenty of privacy. "This is cool as shit!" said Sammy. Shaila walked over and curled up on the air mattress.

We all took a seat either on a chair or on the carpet. Yancy and Temper tended to Shaila as we looked around and made sure we weren't followed. It was still early in the morning and starting to get hotter than was bearable. At least out here it wasn't all desert. There were trees scattered about.

"You guys go on ahead", called out Brett. "I have to use the facilities over here". Everyone smiled because he was referring to a large tree in the distance. He headed for the tree while we all sat down on the side of the bridge. "We need to find out what happened to Tommy and Avery," said Chris.

"I can't seem to grasp what Yancy was talking about. I know he said they must have been bumped out but if that's so, we should have seen two other people standing in their place, right."

"I don't know anything anymore" said Jasmine. "I don't know what time we're in, what day it is, or how long we've been gone. I wonder if my family is looking for me or if leaping somehow wiped out our existence." Realizing what she had just said she raised her hand to her mouth and her eyes got wide.

"What if I, we never existed in our time because we left." She started to cry. Sammy put his arm around her and comforted her. "That can't be possible," he said "If that was so, Avery would not be a fugitive." "Temper's family would not be looking for her." She stopped crying and looked into the distance at the tree Brett had gone to. She expected to see him returning from his potty break, instead she saw three men walking from the tree only one of them was Brett. She grabbed Sammy's leg with a death grip.

"What the..." he looked at her as she watched the men walking toward them with a terrified look on her face. Sammy and Chris both turned their heads and locked eyes with the strangers at the same time.
"Awe shit," said Chris, "That's the guys from the house. The one's that kidnapped me and Brett. They must have been the one's that bumped Tommy and Avery."
No one moved, we didn't want them to know about the hideaway we sat on, or that there was anyone inside.

As they approached, we could see they were holding some sort of gun or stun gun on Brett. "Where is the time capsule?" Asked one of the men. "Where is the mercury bell?" This time his tone was much more threatening and he had some sort of accent.

"Dude," yelled out Chris, "We told you back at the house we didn't know what you were talking about." "You filled the time capsule" the man shouted as his grip on Brett got tighter, "You put it in there. Where is it?!" He shouted again.

Sammy stood up to try and reason with the men but the other one shoved him to the ground with a force none of us had ever seen before. Sammy was a big guy and not easily knocked down.

"Fuck dude! I was just going to talk to you. None of us know what the fuck you're talking about and that's the God's honest truth!" Sammy argued with the strangers. "Think about it asshole, we filled that time capsule years ago. We were kids still in high school. There wasn't technology like that then."

Before Sammy could pull himself up from the ground, the strangers were gone, Brett still standing in the position with his head tilted as if there were still a stun gun jabbing him in the neck.

Jasmine just started screaming and thrashing about. "I can't fucking take any more!!" She yelled. "I want out of this nightmare!" She ran around the side of the bridge and climbed inside and balled up next to a wall holding her head between her legs. Temper came out and said she had heard the whole thing. "What happened to the men?"

"Who the fuck knows," said Chris. "I'm with Jasmine; this is too fucking weird and crazy for me. My mind can't handle much more." He started rubbing his face and rocking back and forth on the edge of the bridge he was sitting on.

Temper raised her hand to her head to shade the sun's glare as she combed the surrounding area with her eyes. I think Brett and Sammy realized at the same time that if those guys bumped out like that it was because someone else bumped in. Hopefully it was Avery and Tommy. They must have been close whoever it was.

Sammy addressed Temper who seemed to know more than we did about how this thing worked. "What is this thing those guys are looking for and who else knows about it? Why would they think the time capsule we buried would have anything to do with it?" She just kept looking into the distance not acknowledging Sammy.

He grabbed her by the arm and spun her around. "Look lady, we want; no demand some answers here. This is not something any of us volunteered for and people are trying to hurt us because of something you know." He towered over her and had no more tolerance for being jacked around but she just pulled her arm loose and walked away from him back into the shelter.

Sammy stood there looking at Chris who was shaking his head in a manner that would suggest he had nothing left to fight with.

Brett followed Temper into the underpass. Sammy sat on the bridge next to Chris. "Correct me if I'm way off base here but didn't we come here to save that bitch? Why are we risking our lives for someone we don't know and worse yet, someone who treats us like idiots? I'm so ready to go home."

"Hey, did I tell you I met a girl in my sociology class today. Yea, we were supposed to meet up after your birthday thing for drinks. Her name is June. I guess I'm not going to make it. Or didn't make it. Hell, I could still make it if we get out of this thing alive, right.

We can go back to when the whole thing started and move forward from there like God intended, right?" Sammy looked down at the ground and kicked away a rock that was near his foot. Chris just looked at him. What could you say to something like that? Tell him things were going to be ok?

We both stood and headed inside to get out of the heat. It looked like Shaila was feeling better, but not good enough to travel or leap. Yancy had a makeshift lab set up in one corner of the hideout. Jasmine had fallen asleep curled up in the corner and Brett was kicked back next to her.

Temper was like a warrior pacing, listening. "Come, sitzen," said Yancy to Temper. "I can't relax, someone bumped in when those guys bumped out and if it was Avery, he won't know where to find us. "Maybe I should head back into town. That was the last place he saw me. He would probably head there."

"Mommy," said Shaila, "Don't leave me. You promised you wouldn't leave me." She put her arms out to Temper who quickly ran to her side to reassure her she would never leave her side.

"I'll go, said Chris. Sammy backhanded him across the arm and rolled his eyes. Damn it, Chris, you know you can't go by yourself. Why didn't you just say me and Sammy will go?" "Maybe I didn't want to go. You just blurt shit out before you even think."
"I'll go with him," said Brett.

"I've been in here too long anyway; I need to get out of here before this confined space makes me crazy. Besides, you need to stay here with Jasmine. If she wakes up and you're gone, she'll lose it."

"Hey, dude, if you insist," stated Sammy. "I could use some down time." He sat down on a blanket next to Jasmine and kicked back closing his eyes. Chris and Brett headed out of the hideout and into the hot sun looking for any signs of weirdness.

They walked about half a mile neither one talking. The sun was high and it reflected off the dessert like a mirror. "Wish we had thought to bring some water with us", said Chris as he broke the mile long silence. "I feel like I have sand in my mouth" Brett gave up half a grin but did not reply.

One more mile and they would be in town and still no sign of anything unusual. They could hear music and children playing as the parade and festival went on.

"We should try and get something to eat and drink to take back with us." Said Brett as if he had been pondering the idea and was thinking out loud. "I'm so thirsty right now my mouth feels like the Sahara."
Chris looked at him and smiled. "I'm so thirsty my mouth feels like a blazing fire in the desert"

"Well, my mouth is so dry..." Brett stopped dead in his tracks and put his arm out to stop Chris. Chris stopped, looking around frantically to see if he could see why Brett stopped.

"What is it?" he asked. "Did you see something?" "Look," he said pointing toward town. "What is that? I can't tell if it's someone dressed up for the parade or if its future cops."

"Dude! Is the sun getting to you? All I see is kids and families." Replied Chris. Brett grabbed Chris by the chin and pointed his face toward the crowd that was barely visible in front of them. "Look!" He yelled out. "Right there! What is that?"

Chris pulled Brett's hand loose and stared with his eyes squinted trying to make out the anomaly. "Oh fuck! It's a big fat man in a suit" he said as he laughed hysterically. "That's probably the Mayor of Sun City."

"Fuck you!" said Brett. "He looked too big to be a regular person." They both had a good laugh and kept walking toward the crowd. The closer they got, the stronger the smell of grilled meats and baked goods filled the air. The parade was over and the booths were opening for service. There was a band tuning up in the background. Everyone was smiling and enjoying the festivities so unaware of the future and how things were going to be in another decade or two. Once you've seen some things there is just no taking it back.

"Ya know," said Chris, "It's weird, I see all these people but they don't even seem like people to me but more like obstacles in a maze that there's no coming out of. I just can't even imagine myself the way I was a day or two ago. Thrasher Land and skateboarding just don't seem to exist anymore. I can't see myself sitting in a classroom or playing tricks on my sister. Even if we get back home, we won't be the same, will we?"

"I don't know, Chris, I just don't know." Replied Brett as they made their way through the crowd looking for anyone familiar or anything out of place.

"We should stop and get something to eat and drink," said Chris. "This food smells awesome!" "I swear all you think about is your stomach. I am really thirsty though. Shit! We don't have any money." Responded Brett.

"I have a couple bucks," said Chris with a grin the size of Texas. "I just found it in my pocket on the way here." He reached into his shorts pocket and pulled out some folded up bills. "How much you have there?" Asked Brett. "Looks like more than a couple bucks."

"Dude, I didn't know that was in there. Shit it's like $120 I had left over from that skateboarding competition! Hell yea! I guess I was wearing these shorts the day I won!" shouted a clearly excited Chris. Mmmm, smell that? Let's get something." Coaxed Chris.

"Well, that **BBQ** looks pretty tasty", said Brett. "Maybe we should go to the store though. We'd probably get more for the money and we could take some back to the others." They stood over a smoking grill looking at the food and debating and not watching their surroundings when out of nowhere a deep and authoritative voice came from behind.

"I hope you have money for that food, son!" Chris and Brett both snapped back to reality and nearly jumped out of their skin as they whipped around only to find Sammy and Jasmine had walked up to the festival.

"OMG! Don't do that!" Brett said as he tried to restart his heart. "You're lucky I didn't turn around and stab you."

"What were you going to stab me with," laughed Sammy. "Jas woke up so we thought we'd head this way and get out of that hide out. So, you getting us some BBQ?

"I just want something to drink," interjected Jasmine. How much does stuff cost these days?"

While the gang was all eyeballing the feast in front of them, they did not see Avery and Tommy walk right past them. They had gone a couple stands away before Tommy heard Sammy. He got Avery's attention and they quickly headed in the direction of their friends before they got lost into the crowd.

They were almost close enough to touch them but were intercepted by a loud robotic sounding voice telling Avery to cease and desist, criminal.

Sammy, Jasmine, Chris, and Brett turned to see
Avery and Tommy about to be shot by a future cop.

"What the hell!" Shouted Brett as they ran with the crowd to escape the violence. Tommy and Avery also ducked into the crowd to try and lose the assassins.
They all ended up hiding out in a car that Avery broke into and was trying to hotwire so they could put some distance between them and the police. It seemed like it took forever but he finally got the car running and he floored it.

"Those were future police weren't they," asked Brett. "Where's Temper?" Shouted Avery. "I think we lost them," said Sammy who was watching out the back window.

"Where is Temper?" Avery asked again. This time with more control in his tone. "How did four of you bump in when only two bumped out?" Chris asked Tommy.

"Damn it! Where the hell is Temper and Shaila!" Avery shouted again. "Someone better fucking answer me!" "They're hiding out in the desert under a bridge," answered Jasmine. "They're OK. We just left them maybe ten minutes ago."

"Where? Show me". Avery demanded. "You have to go back the other way about two miles past the town square," Jas directed "There's a bridge and a wash. They are under the bridge."

"How did those future cops find you? Asked Chris. "Do they have the same technology as you and Yancy?" "I don't know, Chris, that's a good question. I can only hope not. But we have Temper and Shaila now so if we can just get them back to our time, they can see I didn't kill anyone and hopefully they'll leave me alone."

Avery drove while we watched out the windows for the police. It wouldn't be long before they were back on our trail. No one said a word as Avery headed into the desert.

"Just up the road another hundred feet, see it," pointed Jasmine. "That bridge just ahead." "Pull off somewhere and hide the car." suggested Tommy as he quickly glanced around for any kind of cover to hide it in.

There were scattered trees and cactus but not much to hide something as big as a car so they decided to try and camouflage it with sand and bushes they pulled up from wherever they could. When it was fairly well hidden they hiked the hundred yards they were from the shelter.

"Push the bushes aside and they should be inside, under the bridge." Said Chris Brett and Tommy sat on the side of the bridge while the others headed around the side to enter the shelter underneath.

Damn it, fuck!! Shouted Avery as he bolted out from under the bridge. Yancy right behind him. Shaila ist very sick, Avery, Temper did da right ting. She had to get her help. I couldn't take care of her under das conditions. Yancy tried to calm Avery down but he was just about to his breaking point.

Brett and Tommy turned to see what all the yelling was about and saw everyone exiting the hideout one by one with sheer exhaustion and an overall look of disdain.

"What happened?" Asked Tommy with a tone like he really didn't want to know because from the looks of it the news was not good. "Where is Temper and Shaila?" he added. "Please don't tell me they went into town looking for us."

"No, not looking for us," responded Sammy, "Temper took Shaila to her friends hoping to get her to the hospital and let them take a look at her."

"Her condition was deteriorating quickly, Avery, if she didn't do something immediately Shaila would not make it, she still may be critical. Yancy said as Avery could not hold back the tears. He turned and looked at Yancy as he put his hand on Avery's shoulder in comfort.

Everyone just seemed to drop to the ground where they stood and sat with morale at its lowest point since this whole thing started. It seemed inevitably grave and no one dared to even hope things could get better. If Shaila didn't make it, Avery would not only lose his daughter that he adored, there would be no way to keep the police from killing him.

"I fucked up everything," said Avery. "I should never have put Temper and Shaila through this when we didn't have enough research on the side effects. I killed my baby and put my wife through Hell. The police should kill me. I want to die. I, I," he looked up at Yancy with determination on his face as the tears flowed down his cheeks.

"The research," he blurted out, "Do you have it on your disk? The answer is in the research. I remember there being something about organisms that form on the cells when transporting that adult's burn off from accelerated blood flow and..."

"Ya vole!! How did I miss dat!! " Yancy shouted as he jumped to his feet and grabbed Avery's face in both hands and almost lifted him from the ground in excitement. "If we can get her blood flow to accelerate at a higher rate it could burn off the organisms. We never factored in that a child's blood flow goes through the body in smaller vessels and thus slows down. Ohhhh, that's it my friend, we can save her. Get up, get up! Wie need to find your klein kinder and save her life!!"

It was as if God breathed life into all of us as the greatest mind of all times once again broke ground on a new frontier. We all jumped to our feet and ran, not walked, ran toward the car.

Yancy and Jasmine remained at the hideout so Yancy could look further in the research and get exact calculations for a procedure to treat Shaila.

All the men grabbed the bushes and other camouflage materials from the car. Avery jumped in and started it up. He started moving just short of everyone being inside. If the future police didn't pull us over, surely the local one's would as fast as Avery was speeding toward the hospital.

He parked in the emergency room parking and we all ran inside. Avery approached the check in counter and asked if a young girl had been bought in. Before they had a chance to answer he saw the old couple from the festival.

He ran up to them and asked where Shaila and Temper were. They were crying and just looked at him as if they were too choked up to speak. We all approached the old couple and finally the old woman cleared her throat and answered.

"Temper found us at the festival and Shaila was in pretty bad shape. The doctor is with her now but we don't know anything yet. They won't let us go back to see her us not being family an all."

"Where did they take her?" asked Avery with desperation in his voice. He brushed through both sides of his hair with his fingers waiting for an answer. Before the woman could say another word, a doctor came through double doors approaching them.

"Are you the couple that brought in the child?" He asked the elderly woman. "Yes", she replied, "But this is her father." She turned and pointed in Avery's direction.

"I guess you know you have a very sick child there, the doctor started. We're not sure what's causing her illness and not sure how to treat it. Right now we have her stabilized and she's holding on but if we don't find out what is causing her degeneration soon I'm afraid we won't be able to save her."

At that the old woman burst into tears as her husband put his arm around her and pulled her to a seating area.

"My daughter has a rare blood disease and she is being seen by a doctor where we come from and he is on his way." Said Avery, "Would it be possible for me to go see her and my wife?"

As we watched Avery talking to the doctor and the old couple, it was obvious that his family meant everything to him; and at that moment I think we all realized why he took the chance to travel through time in the first place. He just wanted them to grow older being happy in a more carefree time.

He disappeared through the double doors with the doctor at the same time Yancy and Jasmine came into the emergency room. They must have seen him going through the doors because Yancy headed that direction where Jas headed toward us.

It seemed like we were in that waiting room for an hour before we saw Avery come back out. He looked ten years older than he did when he went in. I guess seeing your child that you vowed to protect slipping away and not knowing how to stop it would take a lot out of a person.

We all rose to our feet afraid the worst had happened but not wanting to show our fear. Avery looked up from his daze and said "They're gone." Tears started flowing freely down his face, he made no move to stem the torrent. Jasmine raised her hand over her mouth and started crying as well and buried her face into Sammy's chest. He quickly embraced her. We just stood there staring at Avery unable to speak.

"What was the cause of, you know of..."
Chris was so shocked he couldn't even finish
his sentence. He looked at Brett to finish it
for him. Brett jumped in with "All gone? You
said they." Jasmine still tightly snug in
Sammy's chest started to clinch his shirt in her
fists. Sammy encased her fists with his hands
because he knew what was coming next.

She looked up at Sammy who was
looking into her eyes telling her to calm down.
She unclenched her fists and let go of
Sammy's shirt but turned to Avery.

"They are all gone, you said? What
exactly do you mean by that?" She said in a
calm calculated tone. "You mean they are no
longer in this hospital or something else?"

"They leaped," he said in a low unstable
voice. Jasmine started to hyperventilate while
smiles of relief came to Chris, Brett, and
Tommy who were just happy to hear they
weren't dead.

"Well what did the doctor say?" Asked
Chris.

"They threw me out of there for loitering," replied Avery. "They don't remember Temper and Shaila even being seen in there. Now, I not only don't know if my daughter is alive, I don't know where they went."

"Does that mean someone else came in?" Asked Tommy. "Why, if that happened, didn't someone else go instead of them? Why is it always one of us when there are so many people around?"

"Whoever is already in the leap zone will go first. I can't explain why but that's just how it works." Replied Avery. "Let's get out of here, where's Yancy?"

"Wasn't he back there with you? The last time we saw him, he was heading through the double doors following you." answered Sammy as he put his arm around Jasmine who was just shaking her head back and forth.

"I never saw him," said Avery rolling his eyes to the side as if he was irritated that nothing was going right. "I hope he didn't leap with them, the whole reason for starting this journey was to find him!"

"I thought it was to find your wife and daughter," said Jasmine in a less than understanding tone.

"I was referring to my family and me." responded Avery with an attitude of his own.

"Ok, ok, getting angry at each other is not going to help this situation at all", interjected the always level headed Tommy. "We should probably assume Yancy leaped with Temper and Shaila and we should keep moving since we don't know who came through."

"Oh, you know who came through," said a voice from behind a plant arrangement that divided the waiting room into private seating areas.

"Did you think we were going to just walk away from the bell? You will tell us where it is or you will never see your families again", the stranger from the desert said as he made himself visible and was again holding some strange weapon in his hand.

"Dude, how do you always know where we are?" Asked Chris. "If you can find us so easily and on purpose, you should know where that thing is you think we have."

"Yea," said Brett as he looked at Chris and shook his head in up and down movement, "If you believe it's in the time capsule, take us back to Chris' Mom's house and we'll check it out. You have to take us back to the right time though."

Jasmine took a deep breath and held it in. Everyone perked up a little thinking they may have a way home. You could tell the wheels were turning in Avery's head as well.

The stranger looked past us and until that moment, we didn't even know his partner was standing behind us with the same weapon in his hand.

As we all turned to look, his partner blurted out "Better make a decision fast, here comes the Calvary." And he nudged his head toward a hallway where the future police were headed our way and they had Yancy between them.

"Wait," yelled out Avery but before he could finish the word we were all standing outside in Chris' backyard in 2012, or so we thought.

"The secret police had Yancy!! Did anyone else see that?" Said Avery. "We have to help him."

"He'll be OK" said the stranger. "We need that time capsule. The bell will make your journey a lot easier, trust me."

"Never trust anyone who says trust me" said Sammy. Chris looked around and things didn't quite look the same as when he left home. There had been a fountain in the yard above where they had buried the time capsule.

"Brett", said Chris, "do you see the fountain anywhere? I thought it was near the woods but it's not there."

"Are you sure this is your house?" Asked Jasmine. "This doesn't look much like where we buried that thing. Didn't there used to be a bonfire pit over there?" Jasmine said as she pointed toward the back side of the yard.

"What the fuck is going on?" Interjected Chris. The house looks the same but nothing back here looks right.

"What are you trying to pull?" Asked the stranger. "Is this where the time capsule is or not? We can work together or we can find it on our own, your choice." His words indicated that by finding it on their own, they meant they didn't need to keep any of us alive to do that.

Tommy quickly jumped in and asked what year it was and were they sure they were accurate with whatever they were using to get them where they needed to go.

"We need to get a newspaper to confirm the year," he said. "This could be the house but if it's not the right year, Chris' family may not live here anymore and it may take a minute to remember exactly where the capsule is buried." If it hasn't already been dug up by someone else."

All agreed and started walking from the backyard to the front of the house and then to the nearest convenience store to get their bearings.

Once out on the street it was already apparent the year could not have been right. When they left, the house was brick with a pale pink trim and his mother had flowerbeds in several parts of the front yard.

There were no flowers only shrubs in front of the house and the trim was painted a camouflage green color. The house number was his but nothing else looked familiar.

The trip to the convenience store would take them past Brett's family home as well. They were all curious to see what changes there would be there. When they started to approach the street, you could see the side of the house which was on a corner lot and there were no apparent changes there. The rest of the entire neighborhood looked basically the same as they remembered.

Avery had not spoken a word since the hospital. That was not like him at all. Was he just worried about his family or was he devising a scheme to get the time travel device from the stranger and use it to transport him to exactly where his family was.

It was around three in the afternoon and it was so hot you could cook an egg on the sidewalk. I think everyone just wanted this adventure to be over. You could see it on their faces that they just wanted to go home and curl up in their own beds and sleep for a week.

As they dragged their way to the 7-11 at the corner no one spoke and no one looked up from the ground. The mood was extremely solemn.

"We've got to stop and get something to eat," said Jasmine. "I'm going to pass out if I don't refuel. There's a place across the road up there where we can sit down, cool off and eat and get a cold drink. I think I'm dehydrated."

"That's a good idea" said Chris. "I'm so hungry I could eat a whole cow."

"I'm just really dying of thirst" said Brett. "My little wiggly thing in the back of my throat is stuck to the roof of my mouth." Everyone halfheartedly smiled because they knew exactly what he was talking about. Even the strangers with them cracked a smile.

"I think we can sit down for a bit and relax just as long as no one tries anything stupid," said one of the strangers.

"I have no money," said Sammy, which was typical. He was always broke but never seemed to do without anything.

"Awe man, this time period still uses money," said one of the strangers to the other.

"Don't worry," said Avery. "I'll get you two something to eat and drink."

We all looked at him with some surprise considering these two have been trying to strong arm us since we met them. Avery must have something up his sleeve.

Jasmine looked at Sammy and he at her as they walked toward the 7-11. Sammy kind of nodded his head at her; acknowledging her look and wondering what was on her mind. From the looks of it she was devising a plan of her own.

7-11 had the air conditioning cranked and it felt so good. As they went inside everyone one at a time took a deep breath when they felt the cold air. It was like stepping into heaven from the depths of hell.

They all walked around looking at random items as Avery picked up a newspaper and paid for it. He looked around at everyone scattered about and stepped outside with the strangers quickly behind him.

We lingered in the air conditioning a little longer. Chris, Tommy, and Brett found their way to the same isle Sammy and Jasmine were in and they all looked at each other with wide eyed wonder.

Was this the chance they were waiting for? Could they end the journey here? This was no longer their fight.

Jasmine spoke up first. "Guys, I say we make a break for it. Surely there's a back door in here. We could go home and forget this ever happened!"

"They don't have the time capsule yet. Do you really think they're going to leave us alone?" whispered Chris, "Anyway, this can't be the right time, what's happened to my house? I don't even know if my family still lives in Phoenix. We don't know if the time capsule is still in the yard. How are we going to dig up a stranger's yard and not be noticed? What kind of story can we tell them that would talk them into letting us?"

"Chris is right", said Brett, "As much as I would love to make a run for it and resume my life, I can't see them letting us go without that thing they want."

"Do you really think they're going to let us go if they get it?" Added Tommy. "Let's see what year it is. Then we can figure out what our next move is."

"All of this is your fault," Jasmine blurted out in whispered shouts. "You involved all of us in this so you could claim an invention you will never understand or get your hands on. I told you from the very beginning this would not end well but you just stuck to Avery like he was you oldest, dearest friend. How could you not..."

She started to cry and stopped mid-sentence as Sammy put his arm around her. She pushed away from him and walked away.

All eyes were on Tommy as he started to speak to defend himself but the words wouldn't come. He just hung his head and walked away in the opposite direction of Jasmine.

They both ended up at the newsstand trying to see a date. "2015" said Jasmine wide eyed looking at Tommy. "We're not too far off from the right time. We could make this work, right?"

"Look", said Brett, "The last thing we need to do is start pointing fingers and fighting. We all know this whole fiasco is a mistake and one that we may never come back from but as long as we remain strong and stick together, we might have a chance. No one knows this neighborhood in this time better than us. Maybe we can ditch them at least for a while anyway. Maybe we can find that bell thing and use it to make our own demands."

Jasmine and Tommy had rejoined their group as Brett was finishing up his speech and all agreed to put any blame aside at least for now. He was right, divided we fall as the saying goes. They heard clapping hands behind them.

"Nice speech, now let's go find that bell" said the stranger. How much had he heard? they all wondered as they headed out single file with the stranger close behind.

"You said we could get something to eat," said Jasmine to the man once everyone was outside.

"Well, where's this world famous cuisine," he responded?

"I don't know about world famous," said Sammy, 'But Cheers over there makes really good burgers and wings and the price is more than reasonable," he said as he pointed to a little bar at the end of a strip mall across the street. "I mean, if we were just hanging out and looking to relax somewhere that's where we would probably end up."

"Sounds good to me," said Avery. He gave us all a look that we couldn't quite read but felt like his plan was about to be implemented and wanted us to be ready for anything. We didn't care as long as it was after we ate.

We made our way into Cheers, wow, a few years makes a lot of difference. "I thought we could round up a posse in here and escape," muttered Sammy to Jasmine. "Do you know anyone in here?"

"Not so far," Jasmine replied as she scanned the room. They sat in a booth by a window with Chris and Brett. Tommy, Avery, and the two strangers went up to the bar to order some food and drinks.

Sammy and Jasmine sat across from Chris and Brett staring at them like they were deep in thought and ready to pounce. Chris started to smile as he looked into Sammy's eyes, never having seen such intenseness from him.

"What is it?" Asked Chris. "You look like you either have to take a shit or you're planning something." Everyone looked over at the group at the bar and Jasmine asked, "What do you guys think about getting that bell thing ourselves and using it as collateral to get away from this whole mess?" All eyes turned to her.

"We don't know where that thing is or even what it looks like. I've already been stunned by that gun thing they have and I can tell you it's not the most pleasant thing I've ever felt. They will just kill us and take it from us, don't you think?" Replied Brett.

"I'm still trying to figure out why they think it's in the time capsule," said Chris. "Speaking of that, where is the time capsule and where is my family? What year did you say it was? Why would they move? We've lived in that house all my life. Did we make a list of the stuff we put in that thing? Anyone remember putting any kind of....Oh shit, Oh shit," Chris said as he stretched his arm out on the table with his eyes opened wider than wide.

"I think I know what it looks like. I seem to remember Camry finding this cool looking thing one year in Sedona when we went panning for gold at this riverbed. I remember her saying it tingled when she picked it up and so she kept it.

Now I remember she put it in the capsule. You guys remember, we all put stuff in there that we thought would signify shit we liked. I think that might have been the bell. How would they know it was in there? How could they track it across time?"

"Shhh, here they come," said Brett. "We'll talk about it later. Now that looks tasty," said Brett as they walked up with the food. "I'm about to starve."

We all took a basket of wings and fries with a beer and just looked at each other as we choked down the food trying not to lead on that we now knew what the bell looked like and where it came from.

At least where we first saw it and where it could possibly be now. We just need to find Chris' family and hopefully they took the capsule with them. If not, guess we'll be digging up some strangers' yard.

We could hear the strangers talking in the next booth. They sounded like they had some sort of locator that could lead them to the bell. Avery asked them how they knew about the bell or the time travel.

We couldn't hear everything they were saying but it sounded like they were not from the same time period as Avery and Yancy and that they were from even further in the future.

It became frustrating trying to hear what they were saying and only getting every few words so we quit listening and started making plans on how we were going to get our hands on it without them.

"Ok," said Jasmine, "Correct me if I'm wrong. Camry definitely put it in the time capsule, right?"

"Shhh." Said Sammy as he waved his hand up and down. We waited for a second or two to see if they stopped talking to listen to us but they were in such an involved conversation, we could have said goodbye and they probably wouldn't have noticed.

"Anyway," Jasmine said in a much softer voice as she rolled her eyes in Sammy's direction. "If Camry said it tingled her fingers when she found it, I'm just going out on a limb here but maybe it has some kind of connection to her or something. Or maybe it's just like a magnetic field that surrounds it that they are honing in on. It must not be a strong signal though if they can't just go right to it without anyone's help."

"Are you sure she put it in there?" Asked Brett. "I think I put my football in there. What did you put in there Chris?"

"Shut the fuck up!" said Sammy. "Who the fuck cares what we put in there? All we care about is that fucking bell thing! Focus dude, focus!"

"There's really only one way to find out," said Jasmine. "We have to find it before they do." Everyone shook their heads up and down then took another drink of their beer.

As we watched the door looking for anyone familiar to walk through it, Tommy came with a pitcher of beer from the bar. We all turned and looked at him as if he had lost his mind.

"Are we in here to have a good time with these guys that want to kill us?" Asked Brett. "I'm not really in a drinking mood, dude." Sammy reached across the table and smacked Brett's hand.

"What?" said Brett, "You all feel like this is a party? Those guys beat the hell out of me and Chris in the future. Fuck them, I don't feel like getting drunk."

Tommy sat the picture down on the table and leaned in close. "Have a beer." was all he said and walked back to the strangers and Avery and sat down. They started talking again.

"What the fuck in wrong with you?" Asked Jasmine. "If those guys get drunk, we can take off and find the capsule. They're probably not used to drinking like we are. It won't take much for them to be passed out in the parking lot or puking their guts out. It's hot outside, let's just chill out in here till they get wasted and then we go find out what we need to know about Chris' family and see if Camry knows anything about that bell."

Brett eased back in the booth resting his arm on the back of the seat sipping his beer, obviously not happy about the situation but willing to wait it out at least until it cooled off some outside.

A good hour passed that pretty much consisted of Jasmine looking out the window, Sammy watching a couple play pool and Chris biting his nails.

Brett was nodding off in the corner of the booth by the window.

The pitcher of beer was almost gone and Avery was still talking to the strangers about what they knew about time travel and how much it had advanced from his time.

The strangers seemed to be doing more talking than drinking. Maybe it was time to go to something a little harder.

"Tommy, called out Brett drawing his hand back gesturing for him to step over to his table. Tommy came over and pushed Chris in a bit so he could sit down.

"What's up?" asked Tommy. "I don't think we're going to get them too drunk when they won't drink. We need to speed things up a little. Why don't you go get a round of shots? They'll have to stop talking long enough to drink them. Actually, you can tell the bartender to make ours virgin and there's doubles." He said with a point of his finger and a little wink."

Chris started laughing. "He's been sitting over there quiet for an hour thinking that shit up." Everyone belted out a little chuckle.

"Actually, that's an awesome idea, dude. "Yea, I like the way you think, brother." Said Tommy.

"What's that?" Said one of the strangers.

"Well," said Tommy, "My friend over here just wanted to know if it was ok with you if we did a round of shots. I mean it would look pretty strange if we didn't have a drink or a shot since we are in a bar. We don't want to be kicked out for loitering. What do ya say? Care if I go get a few shots for us?"

"What is that?" Asked the stranger. "Is that some sort of alcohol?

"Well, um, yea dude. In this time, that's what people do in bars. They have drinks or eat and since we ate an hour ago, if we don't do something to spend money, they will ask us to leave plus, it's hot outside and if we have to sit in here until it cools down, it won't hurt to have a drink, will it?"

"I guess not. I don't know anything about shots so you can leave me out of this round", said one of the strangers.

"No, man now that's just rude" said Sammy and everyone at the booth started a ruckus to get him to have a drink.

"Ok, just make sure it's mild", said the stranger, "We have a lot to do later and I want to be able to focus."

"Not a problem" said Tommy. Avery reassured both the men that Tommy was trustworthy and would make sure our business was handled.

Sammy, Jasmine, Brett and Chris turned back around in their seats with much more confidence in their plan now.

"Getting them drunk should be easy after the first one. They won't even feel it until it's too late," said Brett. They all lifted their beer mugs in toast.

The bar is starting to fill up. "People must be getting of work," said Tommy as he distributed the shots to one and all. He held his glass and dedicated a toast to our outrageous adventure.

At first we were all smiles and started to hold our glasses up as well until we thought about what a hard and dangerous adventure it has turned out to be and I guess Tommy realized what he was saying and even he lowered his glass, his eyes and his head.

"That is one fucked up toast", said Brett. "Sometimes I get the feeling you secretly love this whole thing." "How about a toast to finding our way home."

With that everyone, including Tommy and Avery held their glasses up and then down the hatch.

The two strangers really seemed to enjoy the taste of the shot. Ours of course were nonalcoholic. Hopefully they liked them so much they would have more. We on the other hand were staying focused on one thing and one thing only, doing whatever it took to get back to our lives.

Sammy and Jasmine decided to play a round or two of pool while we were waiting around for the sun to start going down. Brett decided he would have at least one shot with alcohol in it. Before we knew it one hour of focus turned into four hours of drinking. We kept telling ourselves and each other that we could drink all night and not get drunk. Well, we all got a little inebriated and those strangers actually turned out to be pretty cool once they put away their stun guns and had a few drinks. Everyone seemed to be having a good time except Chris. He wasn't drinking any shots and just sat in the booth watching the door.

"Dude, want to shoot some pool?" asked Sammy. "I know this is some fucked up shit but we can at least make the best of it. We're only a few years in the future. We can still..."

"Still what?" shouted Chris, "My family is gone! Don't you get it? Either we changed something, fucking around with time or..."

"Or what?" asked Sammy, "Or maybe they moved? We can find them, I'm sure they left a forwarding address or something. One thing is for damn sure, sitting here staring at the door isn't gonna bring them back or fix anything."

"Just go back over there and hang out with your new BFF's." scowled Chris.

"Dude, that's not even fair. I'm over here with you right now because I know you're bumming but there's just nothing we can do about it right now." Reassured Sammy.

Avery walked up and put his hands on the end of the table. "What's on your mind, Chris?" He looked right into Chris' eyes as if he were trying to see the truth behind the words. "We will go back to the right time and you will see your family again. This in here is only to get them to let their guard down. We don't need any more enemies, do we?

They have technology we don't and they can get us back to whenever we want to go. That tells me if we find that bell, this will all be over and we can all go home to our right time with our families.

I don't know if my family is OK or not but I can't think about that right now. I mean, I can't help but think about it but I may never have the chance to see them again if we don't help them. Right now we are all at their mercy so it is in our best interest to get along."

The strangers came staggering up to the table. One of them crashed into the booth with a smile from ear to ear like we were all friends here out on the town. The bar was quite full now and still no familiar faces. The music was loud and the drinks were flowing. Everyone seemed to be having a good time.

The strangers now had names apparently. I heard Avery call them by name. I didn't want to know them. I didn't care what their names were. To me they were strangers and I wanted them to stay that way.

"How do you like alcohol now?" asked Jasmine as she scooted the stranger over and sat down next to him. I looked at her like I expected the others to cave but not Jasmine. "What?" she said as she saw me giving her 'the look'. "Chris, this is Tyler and Jasper." She said in her slurred drunken voice I've heard many times before. "They don't have alcohol in the future, can you imagine?"

"Well," said one of them. I still didn't know which one was Tyler and which one was Jasper and I didn't care. "We have ways of getting pleasure without it." He continued.

"Alcohol was abolished long before we were born." The other said "It was classified a drug along with many other synthetic healing chemicals and replaced with natural methods of pain relievers and intoxicants."

"Alcohol was rarely used any more in my time," said Avery, "So it's not hard for me to believe it is no longer around. Too many problems arose from the consumption of it that it just wasn't enjoyable."

"It's pretty fricken enjoyable tonight, huh Jasper." Said one of the strangers. "I wish we had it in our time." And with that being said he jumped up from the booth almost knocking Jasmine to the floor. She just laughed and ran off with him into the crowd.

"I can't wait to see him in the morning. He won't be enjoying it so much then." Mumbled Chris with a cynical grin on his face.

"Anyone thought about where we're going to stay tonight?" asked Chris. "It's getting dark out and I'm really not into being in here anymore. What are we going to do about finding the time capsule and ending this adventure?"

Sammy and Avery and Tyler just shook their heads and turned away into the crowd to find Jasper and Jasmine. Tommy and Brett were kicking butt on the pool table and not giving a thought to the dilemma they were in. Chris looked at them and wondered how everyone could act like nothing was wrong.

Who were these people? He thought he knew his friends but he did not know these guys. They really didn't seem to care about him at all which wasn't like them. Maybe he should just go out on his own and try to find out where his family was.

Looking out the window next to him he could see the strip mall he used to go to almost daily, was now closed down vacant storefronts and the restaurant across the street torn down was now a parking lot.

Even the Jack-N-The-Box at the corner was closed and had graffiti all over it. This used to be such a beautiful area.

Chris sat watching the traffic at the intersection red light, green light, this side goes, then that side goes.

Oblivious to anything or anyone else in the room his mind wandered back to a previous birthday when he turned eighteen and they had come to Cheers with fake ID's and were going to try to get drunk and were thrown out and banned from a place they had no business being in.

They laughed so hard he thought he was going to bust as they ran back to the neighborhood and to Chris' house. That seemed like way longer than three years. He suddenly felt the strain of ten years in his heart and soul.

He turned and scanned the room looking at all the drunk people laughing and singing and having a good time and for the first time in his life felt completely alone. He slowly stood up from the booth and stretched a little before heading toward the door.

He almost made it too when a familiar face popped up in front of his.

"And where do you think you're going?" came this voice from the past. Not the past he was trying to get back to but further than that. A girl he had met one year when his family had gone camping at Lake Mead.

Her name was Perry but she sure wasn't the little girl he met camping. She had grown up to be an absolute stunning beauty.

Weird to see her in Phoenix. She lived in Nevada when he met her. How did she even recognize him after all this time? Who cares, she was the only sunshine he'd seen since this whole ordeal began. She must be like thirty now, didn't she notice that he was so much younger than her when they were the same age that summer?

Maybe she was too drunk to notice things like that. So many things were running through his head in such a short period of time he had almost forgotten that she had asked me a question.

"Um, Perry? It's Perry, right?" Chris fumbled with his words unable to form a sentence lost in her beauty. "What are you doing in Phoenix? Gosh, how many years has it been?" He grabbed her hands and stretched them out admiring her. "Wow," he said, "you really grew up."

"Well, that tends to happen." She said smiling from ear to ear, elated that she had run into the boy she had fallen so hard for years before. She thought about him all the time and had planned every word she would say if she ever saw him again and now that she was in front of him, she couldn't remember a single word.

After that summer, they had written to each other for a couple years and the letters just got fewer and further between until they stopped altogether. They stood there a while just staring at each other when Sammy, of course, Mr. Radar grabbed Chris by the back of the neck.

"Whatcha doin, little brother?" He asked Chris trying to be cool in front of Perry who was paying him zero attention. "Who's your friend?" he continued trying to set up another conquest for himself. He extended his hand to her and introduced himself.

She shook his hand but never took her eyes off Chris. "I didn't know you had a brother," she said.

"He's not my brother, he's just my good friend. Like a brother. I have a sister, remember Camry? That's my, my, my sister's name, Camry". He felt the lump coming up in his throat. The room started closing in on him. What was happening to him? He never felt so out of control before.

Sammy was talking and there were people all around them but it was like she was glowing and he was some insane mute. He was yelling at himself in his head to pull himself together and try to act like a normal person but her eyes, her hair, her smell, her smile, it was all so overwhelming to him nothing else was getting through.

"Damn dude! What the fuck's up with you?" Blurted out Sammy who obviously saw him turning colors with that insecure hyperventilating fear that comes with love at first sight. He was actually starting to shake.

Perry smiled and tilted her head as she lifted his chin seemingly knowing what was 'up with him'. She felt the same way but seeing his fear she stood strong and covered for him. "Want to sit down", she asked, "Or were you leaving?" "I'm sorry, did I hold you up".

"No," answered Sammy for him. "He wasn't going anywhere." Sammy still gripping the back of Chris' neck shook him a bit trying to force him to get a handle on this thing. He knew how Chris felt, he felt the same thing with Jasmine once. It is really debilitating.

He chuckled and spun Chris around heading him back toward the booth. "We have a booth over here if you want to sit with us," Sammy said to Perry. "Well, I'll let you and Chris get acquainted while I go see what Jas is up to.

"We already know each other, said Chris. We met a few years ago.

"Really?" Sammy questioned. "I don't remember you talking about her."

"Remember that summer that my family went on vacation and we spent almost the whole summer camping? Well, I told you I met a girl there. This is her.

"That story was true?" Sammy laughed out loud, "I thought you made it up. Fuck dude, you never said she was so hot." Sammy looked her up and down like she was naked. Then he slapped Chris on the back and grabbed her hand and told Perry if she ever wanted a real man call him.

Then he went to the bar where Jasmine was arguing with a stranger over the price of electronics or something. He sat on the stool next to her straddling his knees on either side of her stool rubbing her back but watching Perry who was paying him no mind at all.

Perry filled Chris in on everything she had been up to since they last spoke. Not all of it was interesting but he was captivated all the same.

Brett and Tommy wandered over to the booth having lost on the pool table and nudged into a seat on opposite sides pushing Perry and Chris to the insides.

"Guys, this is Perry Ply, an old friend of mine." Chris introduced.

"Wait a minute," said Tommy. "This isn't the girl from the lake, is it?" Chris and Perry looked at each other and smiled now having confirmation that Chris expressed to his friends that he had met the girl of his dreams on that vacation.

"He wouldn't stop talking about you for like two years," joked Tommy poking Chris with his elbow.

"This is *THAT* girl?" Commented Brett "Daaaaammmmmnnnnn! Which lake was that? I need to go there." He joked as everyone giggled.

Brett fidgeted around a bit then jumped up and headed toward the bar. Tommy, although happy to see Chris floating on air had to wonder how he was going to handle this situation knowing they weren't really in a position to start up anything.

He knew this was the only girl he had ever heard Chris talk about. Well, for tonight anyway, he wasn't going to be the voice of reality. He told them goodbye as he got up to head back to the pool table but doubted they heard anything over the beating of their hearts. Hell, you could probably hear that at the 7-11 across the intersection.

As day fell into night, the bar became standing room only crowded, everyone continued to drink.

Even Chris had a couple as he got reacquainted with his childhood love. Avery was not drinking anymore and encouraged everyone to try and sober up. "The sun is down and we need to find that time capsule. This was a much needed and enjoyable break but we all need to focus and get back on track." Avery told Brett and Tommy. "We need to round everyone up and head back into the neighborhood."

Tommy started toward Sammy and Jasmine while Brett headed for Chris.

Brett sat down next to Perry and gave Chris a look that was supposed to let him know it was time to wind things down with his girlfriend and focus on the impending task. Chris returned his look with a scowl rarely seen coming from him. He knew why Brett was there but he wasn't ready for the night to be over yet. He didn't want to lose her again but what was he supposed to tell her?

Brett did a little drum roll on the table with his fingers and left him alone to say his goodbyes.

The others were gathering at the bar to settle up the tab and do a head count. Once they were all rounded up and the bill was paid it was time to resume their mission but Chris was gone as was his girl. They only turned their heads for a second. Everyone looked around the bar. Sammy looked in the men's room, Jas in the ladies room. Not at the pool tables, not sitting anywhere, not at the bar.

"He took off!" Shouted Jasper. "I knew that was going to happen!"

"Let him go," responded Tyler. "We know where the last known whereabouts of the capsule is, we don't need him. Let's head toward that house he used to live in." He looked around at the group and there was nothing anyone could do so heading to the house was agreeable. Anyway, after all the drinking everyone had done, that made perfect sense to them. Maybe that's where Chris went and they could meet up with him there.

They all pushed their way through the crowd and out the door. There were people standing around everywhere smoking and talking but still no Chris.

They started toward the intersection all eyes peeled for Chris. No one wanted to proceed without him but waiting around for him didn't make sense either. The light turned green and they stepped out onto the street when they heard Chris yelling from across the parking lot.

You could still hear the low beating of the music from the bar but Chris managed to get our attention over it. He ran across the parking lot and through the intersection just as the light turned red. Out of breath and all pumped up he was grinning from ear to ear like the cat that ate the canary.

"Dude, you are one scary guy when you're in love", said Brett. Everyone laughed and Chris' face turned every shade of red. "So, did ya get the digits?" asked Sammy as Jasmine jabbed him in the ribs with her elbow. "What do you care?" she asked looking at him with the green monster oozing from every pore.

They cut through the back of the grocery store that was behind a strip mall across the street and went through a townhouse development into their neighborhood waking up every dog between. "How are we going to get into that backyard unnoticed with all these damn dogs barking?" Asked Tyler.

"There's an alleyway behind the house where the trash truck drives through to get trash. No cars go back there and sometimes people walk back there but not too often. We can come in from that way. People around here are used to the dogs barking. They bark at cats and other dogs all night long." Said Chris.

"So," said Brett in a sultry tone, 'What did you do with your girlfriend?"

"She had to stay with her friends but she gave me her number and address." Chris boasted with his chest out. "Look, over there by that birdhouse is the general area I think. What do you guys think? About there?" Chris pointed to a bird house on a pole just about smack dab in the middle of the yard, trying to change the subject.

"Who's got a shovel?" asked Brett. "Did nobody think to grab a shovel? Are we supposed to dig with our hands?" Everyone started muffling a laugh. They were all drunk except Chris who had a couple drinks but not a night of drinking like the rest.

He just looked at them trying to decide if he wanted to guide them and go get a shovel from somewhere or escape and try to help the others after they sobered up. Jasmine fell to the ground laughing while Sammy staggeringly made his way to help her to her feet.

They were all hanging on to each other and giggling, not a useful brain between them. Chris took charge and told them all to hang tight in the alleyway and try not to get arrested while he went and found a shovel.

He slithered along the fence line trying not to be detected by motion lights on the house and made his way into the garage. There was no car in there and the house looked empty at least for now.

He found a shovel hanging on the tool wall and grabbed it. He saw no more reason to hide and exited out the back door of the garage. He could hear everyone talking in the alleyway. "Idiots", he said out loud as he made his way to the birdhouse and started to dig where he thought the time capsule was buried. He had dug down about a foot before the gang realized he hadn't returned and started loudly sneaking down the fence line to find him.

"Hey," yelled Chris. Of course no one heard him since they were giggling and concentrating on trying to be quiet as they tiptoed toward the house single file each one holding on to the person in front of them. Chris raised his hand to his mouth and using two fingers, whistled one loud, long siren. Avery was in front and stopped dead in his tracks with a hand raised in front of him and his eyes opened wide.

The others plowed into the person in front of them laughing out loud. Avery turned around and told them all to be quiet, he heard something. Then they all stopped with eyes wide listening for whatever Avery had heard.

"Oh my gosh, you guys are too drunk to deal with this". Yelled out Chris. "Pull it together, we need to do this while it's dark and before whoever lives here comes home. Is anyone sober enough to dig? Does anyone remember how deep we buried it?"

About that time Tyler started throwing up. Everyone busted out laughing except Jasper who was not only concerned about Tyler but also feeling like he was about to do the same thing.

"What are you laughing about? You poisoned us didn't you?" He grabbed for Tommy but threw up en route.

Jasmine rubbed his back and told him they weren't poisoned, just drunk. It would wear off in a little while.

Chris just kept digging shaking his head in annoyance of how cavalier his friends were being about the whole situation. He had dug about a foot deep and two feet in diameter when Brett wandered over and took the shovel from him.

He looked at Chris with those big brown eyes that were looking like an apologetic puppy. Chris handed over the shovel and sat down on the grass and took a break.

The others were in no way sobering up and they had every dog in the neighborhood barking at them. Why couldn't they just straighten up and be quiet before someone called the cops. That was the last thing any of them needed.

"Who's out there?" came a voice from the house. "Hello?" came the voice again. This time everyone shut up and stood quiet as mice in hopes that whoever was home could not see them just hear them. Then a very bright spotlight came on from the over the back door.

The light was so bright we couldn't see who it was calling out to us but it was probably pretty clearly showing who we were.

"Chris?" The voice said as a back breath. "Is that you? Chris?" She said again. We still couldn't see who it was until she walked out into the yard wearing her nightgown and slippers.

"Jas, uh Jasmine, is that you? Brett? Sammy? What are you doing here? What's going on? Where have you all been? Everyone, we all thought. We never knew." It was Camry, she burst into tears as she ran toward Chris and jumped into his arms. She was older and even though it was only a few years into the future, she looked much older than the last time we had seen her. She was actually the same age as Chris now. He didn't want to let her go and vice versa. He thought he may never see his family again. They did still live here.

"Where's Mom." Asked Chris as he pried her from around his neck but still holding tightly to her arms.

"Where have you been? The whole town looked you all of you for a couple years but you disappeared without a trace. I always knew you'd come back. What are you doing here digging up the yard in the middle of the night?" Camry asked as the questions just kept coming.

Chris gave her a little shake with his tight grip. "Where's Mom? Where is the time capsule?" He shook her again then pulled her close and hugged her like he would never see her again half afraid for her and totally happy to see her.

He just wanted to get that bell and now more than ever get his life back. Seeing Camry brought everyone back to a sudden reality that life is still going on as normal and they should be part of that reality not this hell they had been thrown into.

Everyone gathered close as Camry pushed back from Chris and looked at all of them drunk, dirty and still the same age as the last time she had seen them.

"No, this isn't real" she said. "Am I dreaming? Where have you been? What's happened to you? You all look the same as you did the last time I saw you at Chris' going away to college party. That was years ago. Someone tell me what is going on!" she shouted as she pulled loose from Chris.

She turned and looked back at the house for a second and...

"NOOO!!!" Yelled Chris as everything went black and then his focus returned to see Tyler and Jasper puking their guts out.

"It's a rough one when you've been drinking" said Sammy. "Damn that was rough, FUCK"

Jasmine was bent over like she wanted to throw up but nothing was coming. "Oh my God! That was Camry, she was smiling on the outside but bewildered on the inside.

She looked so grown up. How many years was it? What is she going to do now or think? Is she going to forget she saw us like the couple at the festival or is this going to make her crazy?"

"She won't remember seeing us, said Avery, but she won't be able to explain that big hole in her yard."

"Why did you do that, you asshole!" Yelled out Chris to Tyler. "She could have told us where the time capsule was and then you could have leaped out and left us there! I hate you!!" Chris started to cry and he didn't care what anyone thought about it.

He was fighting mad and wanted his family back. Wanted his life back.

"Dude," Brett reassured his friend, "She won't remember seeing us. If we lingered any longer it's like putting a trace on a phone, you only have so long before you are able to be traced. She would have not forgotten seeing us if we stayed any longer and you heard her.

There was some sort of to-do about us disappearing. At this point, we'll either have to return before anyone realizes we're missing or find some way to resurface with a believable story about why we never contacted anyone in as many years. Preferably the first scenario."

"Well where the fuck are we now and what year is it? Asked an agitated Tommy, trying not to blow chunks out with his words."

"Don't you recognize it?" Said Avery. "Look around, we've come full circle. This is the woods behind my house. Look through those trees, see the back of the house?" It looks like we just made a lateral move. The house looks pretty much like we left it." He started toward the back door when Tyler grabbed his arm. "Wait, I'm getting interference on the spectromagifometer." "The what?" asked Tommy as everyone turned in unison looking at the device he was holding.

"The remote!" Blurted out Avery. He halfcocked a smile and looked at Tyler who wasn't getting the joke. "They call it a remote because in their time they used a similar looking device to change frequencies on their telecommunicator. Tyler just returned a smile as if he really wasn't picturing the concept but he'd take Avery's word for it.

"What do you mean you're picking up something?" asked Jasmine. "Are those time cops here?" "What year is it?"

"It's still 2015" answered Avery. "We didn't move through time, just location."

"I think we're ok, said Jasper. "I'm showing there has been infiltration into the house by the assassins but they're not there now. It's probably just picking up residue. This thing is super sensitive."

"Great, interjected Sammy, let's go inside. I really have to take a piss, bad."

Again Jasper and Tyler looked at each other confused.

"He has to excrete", snickered Avery. "The use of language has changed somewhat from the Ebonics of today. In their time there is one language for all people and there is little slang used for the convenience of proper communication."

They all went inside and expected to see the breakfast still on the table that they had abandoned but the house was clean and there was actually food in the cup boards and the sheet covered furniture was uncovered. Avery and Jasmine slowly danced around from room to room trying to decide if what they were noticing was a timing thing or had someone been in there and cleaned up the mess they all left.

Of course Tyler and Jasper were unaware of the possibilities of the clean house but surely the others had some thoughts on it.

Jasmine was the first to comment. "Is it me? Am I thinking straight to think that this place should be a mess what with us leaving a full meal on the table and the time cops coming through probably ransacking the place?" She looked at Sammy who shrugged his shoulders not having a clue what she was referring to.

Next she looked at Avery who was walking around in circles. Once they make eye contact his eyes grew larger as he ran for the bedrooms to see if anyone was still there. Hoping and praying that Temper and Sheila had found their way back to the house.

It was clearly evident someone had been there and who else would have cleaned and stocked food?

Jasmine ran after him. They went room to room calling out to them while the others gathered in the living room.

"There's no one here." Avery proclaimed sadly as he and Jasmine made their way into the living room with everyone else. Tyler was non-stop messing with the remote. Everyone was feeling a little sick from the drinking, lack of sleep and teleportation. Sammy sat down in a big easy chair and leaned forwards with his head in his hands. Tommy on the couch with Chris and Brett. Jasper kind of slid down the wall and landed in a sitting position where he leaned against the wall and closed his eyes.

"Why don't you give that thing a rest," Avery barked out to Tyler. "Maybe we should get some shut eye and start again tomorrow." He walked up the stairs to his room and shut the door.

"Well, I'm down with that, you coming Sammy?" Jasmine said eyes half bloodshot and looking unbelievably rough for a prom queen.

Sammy looked at Tommy and Brett with half a smile as if confirming that he was still the stud of the group. "You got it babe." He answered as he rose to follow his one-time girlfriend.

Tommy stretched out on the couch shoving Chris to one end with his bare feet. "Sorry dude but this is my spot for the night. Chris didn't say a word: just moved down staring into space like a zombie.

The night continued to move forward in search of the sunrise.

Tommy tossing and turning on the couch, Chris finally had at some point moved into a room, Jasper laid flat out on the floor and Tyler still messing around with the remote.

The sun came up and with it came an intense heat. Days went by and the food was low. Jasper had turned on the electricity at the box so at least there were lights for the time being.

The natives were getting restless and no one knew what to do or what was going to happen. They just existed day to day hoping that any day Tyler would get the remote to do what we wanted it to do. Find Temper and Shaila and Yance so we could go home.

Chapter 4

The Disappearance of Jasmine

Everyone was growing weary of doing nothing day in and day out. No communication with the outside world, no direction, life had just sort of stopped in time. Every day was nearly the same thing, the guys would go outside and throw a football around while Jasmine would watch and Tyler would mess with the remote for hours at a time.

This day was no different. Jasmine was sitting on a blanket in the yard catching some rays still wearing the same clothes she had come to Chris' birthday party in while the guys were playing a little touch football.

It seemed like she had been wearing the same clothes for so long. Tyler was walking around by the edge of the woods talking to himself or the remote or God, who knows.

He started to smile and get excited and headed for the guys to tell them about a breakthrough.

Jasmine sat up watching to see if there was some groundbreaking development that would take them home when all of a sudden she was looking at Temper and Shaila who were inside a jail cell. Jasmine seemed to have leaped but was she in a cell as well? No she wasn't. Did anyone see her? It didn't appear anyone except Temper saw her. Shaila seemed to be asleep on one of the cots in the cell. Temper's eyes opened as wide as saucers as did Jasmine's.

Jasmine quickly looked around in an attempt to find a place to hide. Everything looked so different from anything she had seen before. Temper motioned for Jasmine to hide.

She ducked down behind the desk where she had leaped in next to. "Look around", Temper said in a loud whisper, "What do you see? Are there any police? Do you see Yance?" Jasmine peeked up over the desk looking around a very large room with a lot of desks and computers and cells.

There didn't seem to be anyone around. That was odd. No one at all in this very large room, not even anyone else in any of the other cells.

"Look at the computer screen." Ordered Temper. "Do you see a picture that looks like a pie graph?" Jasmine looked at the computer on the desk in front of her and shook her head yes.

"Ok," said Temper, "That is the cells. From there you can unlock any cell. You have to count from the left to right of this wall, go from the bottom of the pie clockwise and find the wedge that corresponds to the number of my cell. Can you do that?" Temper now half crying to Jasmine.

"Please tell me you understand what I'm telling you, Jasmine, please!"

Jasmine still trying to take in the environment, turned her focus from checking around the room to Temper's words.

"I see the graph," said Jas. You could see her eyes following and counting the cells from one end of the wall to the cell she needed to open. "Ok, I see yours, its number forty-two. I don't see a mouse or anything to click on it with." Jasmine waving her arms in the air.
"I don't know what to do!!" She yelled out in panic. How do I get on it to click it?"

"Jasmine," Temper said in a calm voice, "Calm down, breathe honey, just breathe, OK, ask the computer to highlight wedge number 42. After it is clearly positioned over that wedge, ask the computer to open the cell. If you can get *me* out of here, I can get *us* out of here. I need to tell you that Shaila is dead. She was very weak when they took us from the hospital and she didn't make it through the teleportation process. They just left us in here and she died in my arms" Temper was holding her arms out as if she were holding her.

Tears were pouring from her eyes as she looked at her empty arms. "Please tell me Avery is OK," she whispered through the tears as she pulled her arms tightly around her body and started to rock forward and back.

Jas started to hyperventilate. "Computer, open number 42." then she ducked back down behind the desk. Temper's cell door unlocked and she pulled it open. She leaned over her little girl's lifeless body and kissed her.

With tears flowing out of her eyes like waterfalls, she picked her baby up and ran to Jasmine grabbing her by the arm. "Come on! We have to get out of here!"

The room was divided into two rooms by a wall that came halfway thru the middle of the room, with the opposing wall a row of cells all empty. The two rooms were filled with desks, computers, and interrogation chairs. The lights were so bright and the rooms were painted a sanctuary white.

Jasmine was still trying to catch up mentally as Temper dragged her through the room and out the door into the hallway. The hall was not so bright and seemed to go on forever. What Jasmine wouldn't give right now to wake up to find all of this had just been a terrible dream.

Meanwhile, back at the house, the groundbreaking thing Tyler had managed was he had set the device to locate and retrieve Yance. At least with him, they had a person of extraordinary intelligence to help them find a way to reunite everyone and get home. Little did he realize that by gaining Yance, they would lose Jasmine.

"What the fuck just happened? Where did Jasmine go? You have to get her back!!" Sammy yelled.

"Give me that fucking thing" he said as he rushed up on Tyler and tried to grab the remote from him. Sammy being six foot four towered over Tyler who was sitting in the grass.

He rolled over onto the remote in an attempt to keep a stronghold on it. Sammy grabbed him by the leg and started pulling him across the yard as the others came running to break it up.

"You vill never get Jasmine back if you break der device" came a little old voice from the area where Jasmine had been sunbathing. It was Yance.

He was walking toward the crowd who had immediately stopped in their tracks. "I have good news for you" he said. "I was being interrogated by der polizei in da very room mit Temper und Shaila. Dey ver vondering vas dis kleina device vas. Do you see vat I have here? It ist der bell vie looked for. Now der device can be complete."

Everyone looked at Yance and although they must have heard his words, it was taking a minute to sink in. They were all frozen in place.

Twenty-Five years into the future, just outside of Phoenix, Jasmine and Temper had made their way to the outside which was heavily guarded but the pollution being so bad, they were able to move about somewhat undetected.

Temper was getting weary trying to carry Shaila. She was distraught but hopeful that Yancy would be able to fix this tragedy with time manipulation. Go back to a time before she was dead and not allow things to happen the way they did. Maybe if they could change time, they could change circumstances. Either way, she couldn't leave her baby in that prison. They inched along the building toward the fence and then crept around the fence line to a compromised place in the structure where they could dig under and get out.

Jasmine took off a shoe and started digging the dirt back enough to be able to crawl through while Temper held up the fence wire until Jas was through then put Shaila's raised arms through for Jasmine to pull. Once all three were on the other side, they belly crawled until they were at a safe distance dragging Shaila's lifeless body between them, they crawled until they could not be seen through the dense smog.

It was easily a day or more walk to town where they might be able to locate Yance. His lab was just outside of town. They took turns carrying Shaila and rested often. The heat was almost unbearable.

As Temper and Jasmine sat in a partially shaded trench along the roadway headed toward Phoenix from the detainment center, they both stared at Shaila's lifeless bruising body. The heat was causing accelerated deterioration. They could not continue to haul around a rotting corpse thought Jasmine to herself. She felt she needed to suggest an alternative but was not sure how to say it without seeming callused and unsympathetic.

The tears just started gushing from Temper's eyes as she reached for her daughter and drug her close and held her tight.
Jasmine crying as well knew what was going on in Temper's head and heart. How hard it must be to have to make the decision to leave your child behind when you had such high hopes of being able to save her.

How would she be able to make Avery understand that there was no other choice.

Then Temper lay down in the dirt next to Shaila and curled up around her telling Jasmine to go on without her. She could not leave her beautiful baby in the desert to be carried off by wild animals. She could barely get the words out. "Jasmine, just go and leave me here with her. You'll be alright. I can't go another step knowing she's here in this ditch alone."

"No, Temper, you have to keep going. Killing yourself won't bring her back. You still have Avery and you don't know that Shaila's not still with you in the past. Maybe if you go back..." Jasmine tried to reason with her but the words weren't coming.

"I'm not leaving my baby!!" shouted Temper as she broke down clinching her daughter tighter.

She could feel Shaila's brittle body collapsing in her arms. She let go of her and sat up. She saw that the grip she had on her was leaving bruises and indents on her beautiful child. She knew there was no saving this body, but with the possibility that she might be alive in the past she seemed to gain new hope.

With tears steadily streaming down her face she looked up at Jasmine, "We need to find a way to bury her."

Jasmine nodded her head and started looking around for anything that they could use to dig a grave. She felt so dizzy and dehydrated but knew she had to be strong for Temper. She found a rock that had a flat edge and she bent over to grab it. She started losing focus and thought she was going to pass out from heat stroke.

The last thing she saw was Temper looking into her eyes and grabbing her mouth before everything went black.

Chapter 5

The Way Home

"Jasmine, Jasmine, wake up, what are you doing here?" Jasmine slowly opened her eyes. "Jasmine" she heard again, "What are you doing here? Where have you been? Where is my brother? Jasmine!"

Now the voice was more intense and Jasmine started to focus. She was so dehydrated and disoriented. She looked up and tried to orient herself.

Her hands started feeling the surrounding surface. It felt like grass. It was grass. That voice, it was so familiar.

She tried to sit up but fell back. The next few days were a blur. She woke up in the hospital. There were people drifting about and hospital noises and smells. She could see that she was restrained and had an IV in her arm.

What had happened? Where was Temper? What year and what hospital? She was so confused and felt so isolated. So many things going through her head. Was she captured by the police assassins?

She could see that she must be in some intensive care unit. Her room was surrounded by window. She could see her mom and Camry talking to someone, looked like maybe a doctor.

She had to be back in her own time and home but how did she get there? Was she hurt or paralyzed? There were police in the area. Were they there for her? So many questions. Why doesn't someone come in and talk to her? She thought to herself.

Ok, they're coming toward her room, Mom, Camry and the doctor. Good, no police she thought.

Her mother was crying, and looking at her like Jasmine had never seen her look before. She looked so tired, like she had aged ten years since the last time she'd seen her. Omg! Had had it been ten years? It was all so confusing.

"Where is Temper?" She asked. It was as if no one heard her. Again she asked with more determination for an answer. "Where is Temper? What happened to her?" Again all she got were blank stares from her mother and the doctor who looked at each other as if she were speaking another language. Her mother put her arm around Camry, "Maybe you should go get Sammy or Brett, maybe they could make some sense out of all of this."

"S_S_Sammy? Did you say Sammy and Brett are here?" Jasmine yelled as she tried frantically to get up at least to a sitting position.

As the doctor and Jasmine's mother tried to calm her down, Camry left the room to fetch Sammy and Brett. They took the restraints off of her arms and allowed her to sit up. Of course she wanted to jump up and run to the waiting room but the minute she stood up she fell right back to the bed weak and dizzy.

"Hold on sweetie", her mother told her as she and the doctor helped her back into the bed.

"Is Temper someone's name? Someone you met while you were gone? I'm sorry sweetheart I don't know who that is." Her mother shrugged her shoulders and looked at the doctor shaking her head. "You kept asking about someone named Temper."

About that time Sammy and Brett came into the room. They also looked different. Was she just groggy or had they given her drugs to help her sleep? Jasmine couldn't speak. She just stared at them with her mouth open.

Sammy spoke first. Sammy, who now was sporting a mustache and well-groomed short hair. "Maybe we could speak to Jasmine alone if no one else minds."

"Yes, well, I do have rounds to make," said the doctor, "and Janice, if I could speak to you for a moment out in the hallway, I have some prescriptions for her to fill when we release her."

Jasmine's mother and the doctor left the room and closed the door to give them a little more privacy. Camry, now already graduated from college, leaned in at the bottom of the hospital bed and looked intently at Jasmine.

"Jasmine," she said, "You need to focus. They told me everything when they got back. You and my brother never returned with them. It's been seven years since they returned. We just assumed you were dead until you showed up the other day in my parents' back yard. Chris never came back."

"Jasmine," Sammy interrupted, "Do you know where Chris is? Please tell us anything you can about where you've been. Were you with Chris? Do you know if he's ok or at least alive?"

"Seven years? I've been gone seven years?" Jasmine started to cry. "I was with Temper just before I leaped. That was like a couple days ago right? Seven years? I don't know where, what, I was with Temper in the desert we just buried Shaila." Jasmine put her hand over her mouth and looked up at Sammy with tears in her eyes shaking her head in disbelief. She lay back on the bed and closed her eyes. She rolled to her side and curled up into the fetal position and pulled the cover up around her shoulders almost whispering the words as she told them to leave her alone.

"Jasmine, you have to tell me something about Chris!" Camry cried out slightly yanking on the end of the bed rail. Inside she wanted to yank up Jasmine and shake her and make her tell what she might know.

"LEAVE ME ALONE!!!" Jasmine yelled out as loud as she could and with that the nurse and her mother came running into the room and ushered the others out. Camry resisting the nurse's forceful ejection was frantic for any information however small about where her brother might be.

Jasmine didn't even look at her, she just lay there curled up with her eyes closed. The nurse injecting a sedative into her IV. Seven years she thought. Where was she? Why couldn't she remember? She was so confused. So many questions racing through her head as the sedative started to work.

"She is finally asleep." Her mother said to the nurse. "What was she talking about? I just can't make any sense out of what she says."

"And you may never know," replied the nurse in her slight French accent. "She has obviously been through a lot of trauma and she may not even know if what she is saying is real or a fantasy she made up to deal with some sort of abuse she may have been subjected to.

I'm sorry to sound so bleak about her condition, but I've seen cases like hers before. I think the psychiatrists call it multiple personality disorder. They literally pretend that what is happening to them is happening to someone else inside their bodies so they can sort of project their true selves to somewhere else so they don't have to deal with the torture.

Then they never let go of that multiple personality. Now that she has returned to familiar people and surroundings she may have become confused. I'm no doctor and have no degree to make these comments as a diagnosis but to be sure, you might want to ask the doctor if she can be seen by a mental health doctor."

"Well," said her mother, "That is a lot to think about. I will consider any advice I can get. She has been gone for so long, I just wonder if I'll ever have my little girl back. Right now I think she needs to rest and so do I. If you need me, I'll be in the lobby." Jasmine's mother walked away from the nurse with a heavy heart and a lot of fear.

Fear that the little cheerleader she watched grow into a young woman heading off to college may never return. She headed toward the lobby to discuss with Camry and the others what the nurse had shared.

With so much on her mind, she did not even notice the little white haired man she passed in the hallway heading toward her daughter's room.

No one saw or even suspected anyone could reverse the damage that had befallen the lot of them. This was a sad day indeed for the longtime friends that missed their friends for seven long years only to find that one was still missing and one may never recover mentally or emotionally.

Sammy hugged Jasmine's Mom and Camry then turned to Brett and whacked him across the chest.

"Let's go tell her goodbye and head out. I can't sit here and you have a family to get home to." Brett agreed and they headed down the hall toward the room.

As they were about to enter, they both began to feel a familiar queasiness.

A feeling they barely remembered but could not deny all the same.

As they opened the door to her room and entered, they were sick to their stomachs and yet still had knowledge of the existence they just left. They once again found themselves in that broken down shack with their friends this time, there were a few others also enjoying a birthday party for their long lost friend Chris.

There was Temper and Avery, Tommy and Chris, Yancy and someone they had not met before. It seemed the bell everyone was looking for was the missing piece to a puzzle only Yancy could complete.

"Where is Jasmine?" Asked Sammy, "I understand that we must have leaped back into the time before our journey but Jasmine is still sick and confused. We need to go back and help her!! We can't leave her behind, it's our fault she is like that."

Yancy snickered a bit and raised his hand over his mouth. She ist in sie haus mit us. She ist sleeping.

Everyone smiled and joy filled the room and the house as Sammy rushed into the first room he found to find his love not sick but tired and saddened. She told Sammy about her misadventure with Temper and the loss of Shaila.

How Yancy had found the bell and had been the one who had given it to Camry all those years ago. The problem arose when Avery dug up the time capsule and the bell was misplaced.

Once Avery knew the importance of it, he remembered putting it in this house and Yancy was able to restore us to our original time. He was unable to stop the death of Shaila though.

But unknown to any of us, including Temper, she was pregnant. Now they have a new baby, James, and plan on restoring this house and continuing their lives in our time.

Jasmine and Sammy made their way into the living room and enjoyed a long time awaited birthday celebration with their friend they will be forever bonded with, Chris as he turns 24 once again.

Made in the USA
Columbia, SC
25 February 2019